Searching for Lincoln's Ghost

Searching for Lincoln's Ghost

Barbara J. Dzikowski

WIARA BOOKS

Searching for Lincoln's Ghost

PO Box 11462
South Bend, Indiana 46634

ISBN: 978-0-9840305-0-7
Library of Congress Control Number is: 2011943276

Printed in the United States of America

To my family—
for their real-life lessons in humanity and courage
and the love, support, and inspiration
they bring to my journey

Acknowledgments

First and foremost, I wish to thank my sister, Judy, who championed this novel right from the beginning and who spent countless hours reviewing these pages. Her compassionate and wise heart permeates the message of this story, and her insightful edits were always right on target.

I'd also like to thank Krista Hill for her professional guidance and for steering this manuscript into the hands of editors Elizabeth Day and Stephanie Ernst.

Grateful acknowledgment is made for the use of the following:
"The Prophet" by Kahlil Gibran
"Recollections of Abraham Lincoln" by Ward Hill Lamon
"Abraham Lincoln Walks at Midnight" by Vachel Lindsay
"Let us Break Bread Together" traditional spiritual
"When I Was Young" by Burden/Weider/Briggs/McCulloch/ Jenkins

When I was young, it was more important,
Pain more painful, laughter much louder . . .
My faith was so much stronger then . . .
And I was so much older then, when I was young.

—***When I Was Young*** by Burden/Weider/Briggs/McCulloch/Jenkins, from
the album, The Best of Eric Burden and the Animals, Vol. II, April, 1967

PART 1

Prologue

Yesterday, the small article on the obituary page meant nothing to me. Then, he was merely an "unidentified white male" discovered dead in a parked car in the back alley of a gas station, no one or nothing by his side except an empty syringe needle.

Today, they revealed his name. He was John MacArthur Malone, the first boy I ever loved.

The last time I saw John Malone must have been more than thirty years ago, in high school. Had he even graduated? I couldn't recall. By the time we reached our freshmen year, he was little more than a shadowy, obscure figure I passed in the crowded hallways from time to time, a stranger, even to himself. Already, his face had grown lifeless and angular, like an old man peering through a teenager's eyes, always downcast.

It was not high school but the long days of sixth grade—when the fall of 1966 melded into the spring of 1967—that had emblazoned John Malone's imprint deep inside of me, like an indelible childhood scar. Now here I sat, all these years later, reading a newspaper that disclosed his death, totally unprepared for the gush of long-lidded emotions the revelation was awakening. In dizzying clarity, a parade of half-forgotten images, faces, and places raced through my mind, muting time and its chronological boundaries and evoking the ageless, eternal observer that lurks inside. Ezra would have said that this was the soul making itself known. Maybe it was. Suddenly, I was an eleven-year-old girl again, holding a newspaper with the hands of a woman nearly fifty.

Among the flurry of emotions, not one of them was surprise that John would end up dying in such a tragic way. Even back then—beginning back then—John Malone had been a broken, lost boy. It had taken me nearly the entire year of sixth grade to discover what had made him that way, but discover the truth I had. Accidentally. Together, Ezra and I had learned his horrifying secret.

The sixth grade and all the characters it engendered—John Malone, Abraham Lincoln, and of course, Ezra—had changed me forever. Learning of John Malone's death was resurrecting them, the dormant memories of those powerful childhood days that seemed suddenly like minutes ago, rather than long, lonely years ago. I could almost hear Ezra's explanation: first loves change you, he would say. They rewire you, realign your DNA, create the blueprint inside of you for the love for which you'll hunger for the rest of your life. And it probably was true because only lost, broken men ever held any appeal to me. I guess all along, I had been searching only for John Malone.

He was buried on a graceful summer day, with not a cloud in the sky and a gentle, perfect breeze wafting warmth through the treetops. Still, I chose not to go to his funeral. What would be the point? John would have turned fifty years old a few months after his burial. What could I possibly say to his mourners—that I hadn't seen him in over thirty years and didn't know one thing about the man he had become, only the boy trapped inside of him?

Instead, I decided to linger behind in the cemetery, waiting until the last of the meager group of grievers had driven away, and John's shiny silver coffin sat alone on the grass awaiting its placement in the freshly dug grave. As I approached, a strange feeling seized me. It felt almost as if John Malone's spirit was a tangible presence that had summoned me here. Part of me yearned to pry the heavy lid open and gaze into his face for the first time as a man, to see who he had become. But more than that, I was afraid to violate him that way; I didn't think he would want me to know. As long as his twelve-year-old face was locked inside my heart, John Malone's soul would remain as unsullied as that brave, beautiful boy's once had been.

Underneath the canopy, I sat down on one of the empty chairs erected for his bereaved, none of them (as I had discovered in his obituary) a wife or children. Like me, John had never found a family besides the one he was born into.

And before the grave diggers returned to lower him into the open arms of the warm summer earth, I sat with John Malone one final time, recalling to him—in every detail I could muster—those sacred, unfathomable days of our sixth-grade year.

Chapter 1

"Life is seeds," Ezra used to say.

One of the things I think he meant by that is that nothing is born from nothing. Every story has a seed of a beginning, usually something so small and unremarkable that the chain of events being birthed into motion cannot be discerned until long after the story has taken shape and form. And so it was that the odd events that shaped our sixth-grade story really began unfolding years before the autumn of 1966 when I became a sixth grader. The seed had been planted way back in 1961, when I was six years old, just one year after my parents had been killed on the tracks of the Olive Street railroad crossing.

It was a rather benign discovery at the time. I found it one Saturday afternoon in 1961 while rummaging through the clothes in Mama's closet, which Grandmom had left undisturbed since the day she died. I was searching for one of her sweaters. Wrapping Mama's sweaters around my shoulders was the closest thing to feeling her arms around me again.

Why I didn't discover it before then, I'll never know, but there it was—shimmering under the light bulb in the back of her closet in a small, open velvet box: her amethyst rosary.

I could still picture Mama's contorted face whenever she kneaded the beads between her fingers one by one, her lips moving but no sound coming from her mouth, her eyes somehow looking anguished even though they were closed. I startled her out of her strange reverie once by asking her what she was doing.

"I'm praying, my sweet little Andrea," she had said. (For some odd reason, she had used my full name instead of calling me "Andi," like she usually did.) "And sometimes," she continued, "I use these special beads when I pray especially hard."

I didn't really get it back then. The part about praying, talking to God, I understood just fine. What I couldn't comprehend was the part about needing a necklace to do it. I remember thinking that the rosary beads must be equipped with powerful little microphones inside of them that enabled God to hear her all the way up in heaven.

Anyway, here was her amethyst rosary again, sitting out plain as day in the back of her closet as if she had placed it there that morning, intending for me to find it. I scrunched down inside the closet, twirling the small purple beads between my fingers and examining the little silver Christ on the crucifix, trying to discern the features of his face. But the image was much too small, perpetuating the mystery. I remember slipping the rosary over my head, debating whether I could really wear it like a necklace to Show and Tell, before innately deeming it inappropriate and pulling if off my neck.

Back when my parents were still alive, we never went to church. Mama used to try to talk Daddy into attending St. Matthew's Catholic Church, which was within walking distance from Grandmom's house (where we all lived together). But neither Daddy nor Grandmom seemed to have much use for St. Matthew's, or any other church for that matter. Daddy used to say, "You can pray at home just as good as anywhere else," but the only times I ever heard him pray were during the football games he watched on TV.

Still sitting in the closet, and taking a deep breath, I made the somber decision to use the rosary exactly as Mama had done years before and to start praying on it. I wasn't exactly sure how to begin. (Was "God" his first or last name?) Novice that I was, I began rolling the little beads between my fingertips one by one, contorting my face into as dour an expression as I could manage and moving my lips with no sound. Thus began my first official prayer in what would become a vehement campaign of them.

Grandmom was convinced Mama was in heaven, which was paradise, she promised—flowers and harps and angels and gold sidewalks. Still, she sobbed for her every day and wished her back here with us, in our greasy kitchen on Stipple Street. Our neighbor, Mr. Baxter, said that heaven was a bunch of malarkey. When we died, we died, he said. Sometimes, he'd elaborate about rotting away in the ground and being food for the worms until his wife, Mrs. Baxter, would poke her elbow into his ribs so hard that he made a face like Lee Harvey Oswald when he was shot.

So, you see, I had a very important matter to take up with God; I needed to know, once and for all, where my parents had gone. "Mr. God," I had said soundlessly, "please, please let me know if there is life after death. Please, please, give me a sign."

And that was the seed.

For the next whole year of first grade, I had prayed constantly, massaging the beads until my fingers began to tickle. I prayed as I walked to school. I prayed on the way back home again. I prayed as I trotted to the grocery store for Grandmom, to fetch a bottle of milk or some other forgotten item on her shopping list. I prayed at night, as I waited for that sleepy feeling to whisk me away into faraway lands and secret places.

I'd look for God's answer everywhere—in my dreams; in the clandestine codes in the cracks of the sidewalks; in the clouds, where I searched for revealing shapes.

And after all that vigilant praying, I finally got an answer: one solitary, distressing dream.

In my dream, I was upstairs in my room, asleep in my bed, when suddenly, I couldn't catch my breath. Arms flailing, I scrambled to find the glass of water on my nightstand and frantically gulped it down. Well, that only made it worse, because I started choking on the water. I gasped and gasped, but I couldn't catch my breath, no matter how hard I tried. I felt like I was drowning! It was the exact same feeling as the day I had nearly drowned in Lake Michigan the summer before my parents died, and Daddy pulled me out of the water. I had thought I was a goner then, but he saved me, and now here I was—drowning all over again in my dream, this time from a stupid glass of water! I felt a shrill swooshing inside of my head, like the time Dr. Mosby had shot my head full of water to flush the clogged wax out of my eardrums. In my dream, I could still hear the usual noises happening around me, like the radiator banging in my room, but they became increasingly muffled compared to the horrible gurgling sounds inside of my head, as if all my organs were being sucked out through my ears. It went on like that for a while—my hearing both worlds at the same time—until finally, the slogging between my ears completely submerged all other sounds. I kept trying to yell for Grandmom to come rescue me, but I couldn't get any words out at all. Finally, I must have drowned because everything went completely quiet and black. I felt lost and utterly alone.

That's when I woke up, backward and bolt upright in bed, screaming hysterically for my mother's arms, but only the darkness held me. And that's when I knew that death was the end of it all, just like Mr. Baxter had said. No harps and angel wings. Just worm food and a great big nothingness.

I would have been *certain* there was no such thing as life after death, just like my dream revealed, if it weren't for something that happened to Janine Langendorfer, my neighbor three doors down, just two years later, in 1963, when I was a third grader and she was a sixth grader. Even though I had long stopped praying for a sign by then, I couldn't help but wonder whether Janine's experience was some kind of a delayed response, especially since one of Grandmom's favorite sayings was "God may not be swift, but He's always just."

Janine Langendorfer astounded the entire school by claiming that she had seen the ghost of Abraham Lincoln on a rainy Thursday afternoon in late November 1963, the day before President Kennedy was assassinated. That afternoon, all grades, kindergarten through sixth, had performed—in ascending order—for the Thanksgiving program in the school's gymnasium/auditorium. Janine was walking home from school when she realized she had left her pencil box behind the stage after the sixth graders' grand finale, and so she turned around and trotted back to the school and up the dark steps to the auditorium. Stepping onto the stage, she pulled back the heavy velvet curtains, and that's when she saw him: Abraham Lincoln, deep in thought, standing in front of the dormer window with his hands clasped behind his back, inches from where her pencil box rested on the floor.

There was no way of mistaking that it was Abraham Lincoln, Janine had said, because he was wearing his stovepipe hat and black, long-coated, broadcloth suit, with a clumpy knotted bow tie beneath his chin. His torso wasn't much larger than any other man's, but his long, thin legs looked like a sculpture gone wrong—as if someone had stretched his legs out disproportionately until it was too late and they had hardened that way. From beneath his hat, his black hair was sticking up in all different directions, she said, thick and course as a horse's tail.

As she had stood there aghast, her feet bolted to the floor, Abraham Lincoln slowly turned around to look at Janine Langendorfer. He was all wrinkled and discolored, she told us, with a big bump on his right cheek, near his lips. His nose was huge, his eyebrows overgrown. Yet even with all that, she said he looked more sad than scary.

She swore she'd never forget Abraham Lincoln's eyes as long as she lived. Nestled between dark eyelids and craggy, lined skin, Lincoln's eyes sat like two shining gray lights, the same color of pure gray as a foggy spring sky.

That was the part that made me halfway believe Janine's story; she wasn't creative enough to conjure up a detail like that all on her own. The stovepipe hat and kindly, careworn face, we all knew from our history books and the countless Lincoln portraits that lined the hallways of our school. But *gray* eyes? Who had ever seen gray eyes before?

Of course, Janine had her doubters—mostly the parents and the teachers—who believed that she was an overly imaginative little girl who made up the whole story to explain the missing pencil box to her frugal mother, the longtime treasurer of the PTA. But wouldn't any mother, however thrifty, rather have her daughter come clean about misplacing her pencil box than have her be known for the rest of the school year as the wacky little girl who thought she saw Lincoln's ghost?

As far as we kids went, Janine became somewhat of a hero after the sighting. We might have thought she was a wacko too, but truth be told, she had history on her side; she wasn't the first student to see Lincoln's ghost appear in our school. Sooner or later, all the students became acquainted with the Lincoln Legend.

As the tale went, way back in 1938, a sixth-grade boy named Elias Morton swore that he saw the ghost of Abraham Lincoln standing at the top of the stairs leading to the auditorium, his long arm outstretched with an extended index finger wagging toward Elias, as if warning him, "Don't come any closer." Terrified, Elias fled to summon the nearest teacher, who returned with him to the staircase. The teacher never saw Abraham Lincoln, but she did see smoke coming from the closed doors of the auditorium and immediately pulled the fire alarm. The whole school got out in time before anyone was harmed, but the four-alarm blaze burned away three-quarters of the roof, and the attic and auditorium/gymnasium were gutted. Except for the part about Lincoln's ghost, the incident was well documented in the old local newspapers.

One time when we were talking about it during recess, I wondered aloud why Lincoln's ghost seemed to appear only to sixth graders. My best friend, Alfreda, thought it was because Lincoln's favorite son, Willie, had died when he was eleven years old, the same age kids are when they begin the sixth grade.

That sounded like a plausible explanation to me, but Grandmom had one of her own. She said it was because sixth graders have too much pent-up energy that travels up to their heads and causes them to imagine all kinds of weird things. She liked to compare sixth graders to bugs that burst out of their shells, metamorphosing into an odd, in-between place where they're too old to be children and too young to be anything else.

Jimmy Smithers had called me a liar when I shared my dream on the playground once in the third grade. "You didn't really dream you died," he had said in that smug way of his, like he knew everything about everything.

"Uh-huh," I had retorted.

"Nuh-uh," he had shot back. "If you dream you die, you really die. So if you really died in your dream, you'd be dead right now."

It might have been a logical argument, but Jimmy Smithers had been a pea-brain since I first met him in kindergarten, and I told him so. Though I secretly hoped he was right, regrettably, he never was. In his oral history report the week before, he had informed us that the presidential faces on Mount Rushmore were created naturally by Mother Nature.

Those two Lincoln sightings were the only things I had to hang onto for any shred of hope about life after death. If death really was the end of everything, like my dream told me it was, I just couldn't explain how Abraham Lincoln kept showing up in our school auditorium.

I guess I thought about death and dying far too much for an eleven-year-old girl, probably because my Grandmom seemed to think about it constantly. She had been raising me since that November night in 1960 when my parents had gone out to celebrate John Kennedy's election to the presidency. There had been a big celebration bash at the old Marchant Hotel in downtown Castalia. My memories of that night—the last time I ever saw my parents—were vivid. Mama had looked like a movie star in her long, scarlet evening gown with sparkles on her sleeves, and my daddy was so dashing in his shiny black suit. Daddy had swooped down to pick me up and plopped me on his lap, and Mama scolded him for wrinkling his rented suit in the process. But he kept me there anyway, whispering that I was the prettiest thing he'd ever seen. Of course, I knew it wasn't true, but I loved to hear him tell me anyway. In truth, I was just a plain, nondescript kid, brown-haired and brown-eyed, who easily got lost in the shuffle in my kindergarten class. Though I raised my hand a lot, Mrs. Carter seldom called on me, and whenever she finally did, she called me "Annie" instead of "Andi."

On their way home in those fancy clothes, my parents had halted our Studebaker in front of the guardrail at the Olive Street railroad crossing, where the red lights flashed for more than six minutes (the newspaper later reported) without one sign of an oncoming train. A long line of cars was accumulating behind them. Finally, Daddy got tired of waiting. As he maneuvered our rusty pink-colored car around the guardrails, the train suddenly slammed through the darkness like a hurricane. They were both killed instantly.

Grandmom never did recover from my mommy's death, and she never forgave my papa for his decision to disregard the guardrails. Even six years later, she still cried half the time and talked about death the other half, reveling in the details of their dying as if keeping the pain alive was her way of keeping my mama alive. She sometimes reminded me how beautiful Mama looked laid out in her coffin in her silk silver dress, a vision I needed no reminiscing about to remember on my own. (Daddy's body had been too smashed up for an open coffin.)

When I came home from school, more afternoons than not, I found Grandmom sitting at the kitchen table clutching my mother's high school graduation picture against her breast and sobbing, "My poor Mary Jane, my poor Mary Jane."

"I want you to bury me in this color when I die," Grandmom used to say whenever she wore her flowered housedress, which was often, pointing to the smallest petals in the fabric design, the little lilacs. I used to be terrified that Grandmom really would die and leave me too. Sometimes when she napped too long in the big, soft living room chair with the fringed blanket, her head back, her mouth gaping, I feared that she had died in her sleep. I would stare at her, watching for movement of any kind. If none came, I would tiptoe over to the chair, staring closer and closer into her face, listening for the reassuring rhythm of her breath.

She always waited until I got about as close to her face as any human could get before she popped her eyes wide open and said, "Cockadoodle doo!" Of course, I sprang back ten feet every time, in startled and relieved surprise. Then we'd laugh together, comforted and grateful we were still alive. She loved that game, that moment, because it was one of those times when she still was able to outfox death.

The old Lincoln Elementary School—or Stinkin' Lincoln, as most of us called it—was erected on a site that straddled a boundary line. It was not a visible boundary line, yet it was a demarcation that all of Castalia, Indiana, was well aware of. On the right, or to the north, was the white neighborhood, and on the left, to the south, the Negro neighborhood. Grandmom liked to say that the school was appropriately named for the Great Emancipator, since the student population was half-Negro and half-Caucasian.

Actually, it wasn't always that way. Way back in 1908 when the school was first built, it had been an old country school, far too big for the community's needs. But by 1922, it was already regarded as overcrowded. Back then at the turn of the century, it wasn't colored kids who half-populated the school but white immigrant children who couldn't speak much English—mostly Polish and Hungarian kids. I knew all of this only because Grandmom attended Lincoln when she was a little girl, and she told me so.

But that was then. "Time marches on," Grandmom said, in that dramatic way of hers, "and as the old oppressed slowly rise to the top like cream, the new oppressed come to take their place." She waved her hand upward like a dancer whenever she said that, and I always thought that she was describing steam more than cream.

For the most part, I learned how to decipher Grandmom's complex way of thinking. After my parents died, Grandmom developed a kind of split personality: she was either happy or morose, stern or childlike, neglectful of me or overprotective, but never anything in between the two extremes. She leapt from one end of the mood spectrum to the other, leaving me puzzled as to which Grandmom would emerge at any given moment.

During her attentive days, we went walking together, savoring the familiar peculiarities of our old neighborhood—like the Baxters who came out every evening like clockwork to perch together on their front porch swing, always seeming angry at each other; or the uneven cement sidewalks that one of us usually stumbled on; or Mr. Slaby's fat, old poodle Pom Pom plodding to the corner fire hydrant all by himself every single time he had to pee; or the fine yellowing lace curtains hanging in Mrs. Quimby's huge front picture window. Sometimes, Grandmom and I played games together as we walked, counting Chevrolets or seeing which of us could spot the most blue jays and cardinals, the winner earning a dime from the other. Grandmom always carried a shredded, used Kleenex in her pocket that she'd whip out at will for various purposes during our walk—such as blotting either of our runny noses dry, discarding a sour lemon drop, or wiping away a sudden tear if something reminded us of Mama.

When we finally strolled past old Lincoln School, Grandmom always stopped, pausing long enough to share stories with me about her own school days there, including the one about the Hungarian boy with the dirty neck whom she had sat behind in the sixth grade. The way she smiled whenever she told the story, I suspected she was remembering more about that boy than his dirty neck. But she never told me the rest of the story.

The old school looked like a structure from a gothic fairy tale. The worn copper-colored bricks rose up into curlicues and scallops, and the two dormer attic windows peeked out on either side of the green slate roof like giant frog eyes. A rickety fire escape crawled up the length of the building on both sides of the school.

Lincoln School never seemed more like a boundary line than it did during the long summers. Though my best friend since first grade, a Negro girl by the name of Alfreda Phillips, lived only nine blocks away—she lived four blocks to the left of Lincoln School, and we lived five blocks to the right, on Stipple Street—white kids never ventured to the Negro side of Lincoln and vice versa. Not for any real reason that I knew of; it simply wasn't done. During the long summers, Lincoln became a mighty wall that separated Alfreda and me. But when autumn eventually returned, the school collected us again like socks of all colors tumbling happily together in a giant brown-brick dryer.

I could hardly contain my excitement about starting the sixth grade that coming fall of 1966. Grandmom fueled that excitement. She told me that it would be the most important year of my life, whispering that information during our summer walks as if she had been entrusted with some secret vision.

Though Grandmom had more than her share of visions and premonitions, she never believed that Lincoln's ghost haunted the school. She conjectured that Janine Langendorfer simply had consumed too much sugar on that fateful day, and that's all there was to it. If Abraham Lincoln was going to linger on this earth, Grandmom rationalized, why in the world would he be hanging around an elementary school in Castalia, Indiana? He'd be off haunting a location more befitting, like the White House, appearing to President Johnson and advising him on what to do about the Vietnam War or civil rights, not frightening Janine Langendorfer from retrieving her pencil box.

Though I could always tell Grandmom most anything, that summer of 1966, I didn't tell her that I was starting to pray on Mama's rosary all over again. This time, I was praying to be the next sixth grader to see Abraham Lincoln's ghost—not only see him, but talk to him too.

I had to know, once and for all, if there really was life after death.

Chapter 2

When I opened my eyes that morning, there he was—George Harrison. Waking up under George's scrutiny was a new thrill. Just last week, Grandmom had purchased the gigantic poster for me to celebrate the beginning of my final year at Lincoln School. The poster had been created from an old photograph shot back in the days when Beatlemania was still brand new. George was posing with John, Paul, and Ringo, all of them wearing light tan suits without lapels, and all of them grinning, except for George, who rarely smiled. That was why I liked him the best—his eyes harbored deep secrets the rest of us could not fathom. Was it any wonder that George composed and sang my favorite Beatles tune of all time, "Do You Want to Know a Secret?"

It was September 6, 1966, the Tuesday after Labor Day and the first day of sixth grade. Soon, I would be joining the rest of my friends in Mr. Jackson's classroom on the second floor, where we would embark together on that long-anticipated journey of reaching the pinnacle, the top grade of the entire school! I could hardly wait to see Alfreda again.

She and I had been best friends forever, since way back in the first grade after we discovered we had so many things in common. It was almost spooky. For starters, our first names both began and ended in A and our last names started with a P; my name was Andrea Powell, and her name was Alfreda Phillips. She was named after her father, Alfred, and was being raised by her grandmother. Her parents weren't killed like mine; they just simply vanished one summer day when she was still in diapers. I guess that was both a good thing and a bad thing for Alfreda—bad because it meant they opted to leave her behind, good because she still harbored hopes that they might one day return.

My outfit, carefully selected and reselected about a dozen times over the past few days, was hanging on my closet door: white cotton blouse, gray pleated skirt, and white go-go boots, just like the dancers on the TV show *Hullabaloo* wore. Grandmom had given me the boots for my eleventh birthday. I wanted to wear fishnet stockings, like Twiggy, but Grandmom quickly put the kibosh on that. Maybe on graduation day, she said, but not a day sooner.

After a huge breakfast of scrambled eggs in butter, pan-fried potatoes, and bacon—and a greasy kiss from Grandmom—I left out the back door to begin the short walk to school. As soon as I reached the corner, I spotted other kids—some alone, some in groups, big ones and small, carrying book bags and paper-bag lunches as they stepped carefully over the uneven sidewalks in their stiff new school shoes. Some of the girls, like me, sported ponytails. As for the boys, their hair was all pretty much the same, shaved close to the scalp, as if they had just escaped from the barber's chair.

In a little less than ten minutes, Lincoln School was in my sight. All summer long, it had stood alone and forsaken, like a vacant warehouse. Now life was buzzing all around it, with children flocking from all corners of the neighborhood, patrol ladies standing vigil on the street corners with their bright orange sash-bands, traffic jamming as parents dropped their children off at the curb, and the teachers standing on the top of the steps by the front door, trying to bring a semblance of order to the chaos.

I spotted some of my classmates lining up in front of Mr. Jackson, who was checking off names from a list as each new student joined the line. He was wearing dark-framed half-glasses, peering over them with a stern, concentrated gaze. These same kids and I—give or take one or two who were added or subtracted each year—had been in class together since kindergarten. I knew every single one of their names, all of their quirks, and all of their attributes. Already standing in line were Jimmy Smithers, Betsy Talmidge (who was wearing nylon stockings!), Wanda Sims, Bobby Karczewski, and Lorraine Dolezal, and finally, there talking with the twins, Jocelyn and Linda Lee, was Alfreda too!

I ran to Alfreda and threw my arms around her neck and then took in her new appearance with an approving gasp. Gone were the tight, tiny braids all over her head, locked in place with assorted colors of barrettes. During the summer, Alfreda had trimmed her hair into a short haircut, close to her face. She looked like a sixth grader now, suave and sophisticated.

Next it was her turn to size me up. "Oh, girl, your boots are so cool!"

Other than one new teacher and the bumper crop of kindergartners, the rest of the crowd looked pretty familiar, some in more vague ways than others. The new teacher resembled a Ken doll, dimpled and immaculately dressed in a navy sport coat with gold buttons, his thick hair the color of sunflower petals. He was trying to organize one of the lines of the littler kids. I gave Alfreda a nudge and asked, "Who's *that*?"

"That's the new third-grade teacher, Mr. Alphonse," she informed me with a starry-eyed nod of appreciation. "Mrs. Williams retired over the summer."

Just as we were starting to catch up on our news, Mr. Jackson moved over to where I was standing and motioned for me to step out of the line with a beckoning curl of his long index finger.

"Welcome back to school, Andrea," he said, clearing his throat in that cursory way adults do when they're about to tell you something unpleasant. "I'm afraid that you won't be in my sixth-grade class this year, Andi," he said, without a smile. "It appears you've been reassigned—to Mr. Banner's sixth grade."

What? He might as well have whacked me in the head with a ball bat. Alfreda's mouth flew open. I could feel the blood gushing into my face; the chaos around me was swirling into slow motion as I tried to absorb the news. "Mr. Banner's class!" I said, not certain if I was thinking the words or shouting them out loud. "But why?"

Mr. Jackson laid a heavy hand on my shoulder, comforting me. "You know I'm not the one who makes these decisions, Andrea," he said. He cleared his throat again.

"There must be a mistake then!" Alfreda said.

He looked over his list once more, but I could tell he was indulging her. "Nope, no mistake. Andi's not on my list." His voice dropped a little, in both volume and octave. "Look, Andi, they decided to mix things up a little this year. There'll be a few other kids from your old class, so I'm sure you'll be just fine . . . See?" he said, pointing suddenly. "Carol Miller's been transferred too."

I looked over at the line where Mr. Banner was standing with pursed lips, emaciated and frail in his tweed jacket, as if the draft from passing cars could level him to the pavement. He was checking off names from his class list in an elaborate gesture that looked more like he was threading a sewing needle. Carol Miller was standing in the back of the line, eyes full of horror. As she watched me step out of Mr. Jackson's line and approach her, a faint, relieved smile softened her face. Behind me, I could hear the muffled sound of Alfreda's voice as she pleaded to get herself changed to Mr. Banner's class too.

I felt like I was watching my own body from a distance, curious as to which would gush out first—vomit or tears. Maybe both. Slowly, I took my place in line behind Carol Miller. Everyone knew she was a whiner and a snitch, but at least she was someone safe and familiar.

"Oh, Andi! How could this happen?" she asked.

It felt like a bad dream, as bad as my death dream. "I don't know," I said, shrugging, "but I'm gonna get Grandmom to look into this."

"I'm afraid, Andi!" Carol moved close against my ear and lowered her voice to a whisper. "This is the sixth-grade class for the dumb or mean kids."

She didn't have to tell me what I already knew, but now that she had gone and said it out loud, I felt even worse. I nodded, my stomach churning new knots. Big Bernard Wilson, nearly a man now, was pushing and shoving a boy at the head of the line. This would be Bernard's third shot at the sixth grade. His upper lip was already sprouting the vestiges of a mustache.

Numbly, I scanned over the faces of the other kids standing in our line, one by one. Most were very familiar. However, except for Bernard, who everyone knew, I had no clue what any of their names were. In lieu of names over the years, my classmates and I had mostly just described them when we talked about them, like the mulatto boy who was half-Negro and half-white, the tall girl with the tiny head, the kid with the cleft palette, or the scary-looking, colored girl with jagged teeth who looked like someone had thrown a beer bottle into her clenched mouth.

Not everyone in Mr. Banner's class was some kind of freaky mutant. The ones who looked normal were odd in other ways—slow learners, kids with discipline problems, or maybe just the newest kids in school, like the light-skinned, colored girl near the head of the line who I was certain I'd never seen before. She had her hair straightened into a flip, just like Marlo Thomas on *That Girl*.

Toward the front of the line, I spotted the only other kid from my old class—Howard Taylor, a diminutive Negro boy, quite possibly a genius, and he looked the part. He always wore a bow tie, cardigan sweater, and socks to match. Seeing him there gave me some solace. If they transferred the smartest kid in our class too, I couldn't have been shifted to Mr. Banner's sixth grade because they thought I was stupid. So, why *was* I reassigned?

As the school bell clanged, we began our slow march into the school, line-by-line, grade-by-grade, starting from the kindergartners on up. My mind remained in a stunned fog as our line began to move through the glass doors, up the wide flight of stairs just inside the building, and across the hardwood floor to two flights of steps with lacquered wooden banisters. The school had its usual distinct smell, which provided some small comfort. Not exactly a musty odor, it was an indescribable mixture of wood, cleansers, and dusty books mingling with the scent of percolating coffee wafting up from the big urn in the basement where the teachers went to fill their mugs before class started.

Once on the second floor, we passed another of the umpteen pictures of Abraham Lincoln lining the walls; in this one, a bespectacled Lincoln was seated in a chair with an open book as his youngest son, Tad, stood beside him, both of them looking down at the pages, as if Abraham was reading to his son.

Mr. Banner's classroom was the middle room on the left of the second floor, featuring the only fire escape exit door on this side of the building. There were five neat rows of desks, all of them with wooden tops supported by light steel frames and openings large enough to store our textbooks, now stacked on counters in the back of the room, waiting to be disbursed. Behind Mr. Banner's large gray steel desk at the front of the room, an American flag hung on a wooden pole. A large calendar with pictures of all the presidents was posted nearby, with the biggest picture at the top being that of the current president, Lyndon Johnson. On the right side of the room was another portrait of Abraham Lincoln looking dull and sad, his left eye floating slightly upward into his head.

Mr. Banner instructed us *not* to sit down "wherever we so pleased" because he was going to be assigning seats. A groaning protest followed. Mustering a firm "quiet, please!" he began the dreaded process of arranging us in alphabetical order.

One by one, I watched each student claim their assigned desk until Mr. Banner finally got to the Ps, and my own seat beckoned. Mr. Banner's nose twitched slightly as he read the next name, pointing at the desk behind my own: "Bertha Riggs."

So Bertha Riggs was the name of the snaggletoothed colored girl. She plopped into her seat and promptly yanked my ponytail, sniggering through her jagged teeth. The sudden movements stirred up her body odor, a sickly, sour smell like spoiled milk or rotten eggs. Though she had pulled my hair hard enough to make my scalp sting, I pretended not to notice.

Now that I was seated, and the shock of being transferred was wearing off, my mind was beginning to function again. This was *not* a bad dream; this was *really happening.* What on earth was I going to do?

Carol Miller's desk was an aisle away from mine, toward the front. At recess, I'd find her, and we could huddle together on the playground to formulate a plan. Surely, if her mother and my Grandmom got together to protest our placement in Mr. Banner's class, Principal Mortenson would have no other choice but to retract his decision to assign us to this snake pit.

Chapter 3

As it turned out, Grandmom's split personality kicked in when it came to my being reassigned to Mr. Banner's class. At first dismayed by the news, she paced the kitchen like a bloodhound on the scent of a predator, practicing the diatribe for her confrontation with Principal Mortenson. But later, even before she met him in his office the following day, she started losing interest in the injustice of my plight. When she finally did return from her trip to Lincoln Elementary, it was with a sigh and a little speech about making lemonade out of lemons.

"But did he say *why* I was put in Mr. Banner's class?"

Grandmom sighed again. "You know, I asked him that very question," she said. "I asked him, point blank, 'Why Andi?' And do you know what he said? He said, 'Why not Andi?' They simply wanted to mix the classes up, and *someone* from the one class had to move to the other. It was all pretty much a roll of the dice. It wasn't because you weren't special enough, and it wasn't because you were too special; it was a random decision. And frankly, sweet pea, that's just the way life happens. We're all victims to its senseless whims."

With that philosophical explanation, my fate was sealed. In the court of Grandmom, there were no appeals.

Secretly, however, I wondered if Principal Mortenson had really told her something else too horrible to share with me because she was smiling at me with her headache expression and rolling her fingertips over her temples. I knew what it meant; it was always the first sign. Her headaches meant she was retreating to an odd place inside of herself where she vanished for weeks at a time, every now and then, abetted by the dark brown glass bottle in the top cupboard with the Geritol label on it. Her medicine, she called it.

I'd seen her pour as much as a whole glass at once, other times just a spoonful or two. She must have had big refill jugs stashed somewhere from which she'd replenish the original bottle because I never actually saw her buy Geritol when we went shopping. During her Geritol days, she didn't sob over Mama's graduation picture, which was a good thing. Sometimes she would even sing Perry Como tunes when she was washing the dishes. But the bad part about it was she didn't seem to notice me much on those days; it was like her mind went on vacation from her body. She'd stare at me from across the table while we chomped away on our dinner, but I could tell she wasn't really seeing me at all; she was seeing something or someone else in her mind's eye. Though I could reach out and touch her cottony gray hair, she was a trillion miles away from me.

Sometimes I'd even test her, just for the heck of it. I'd say crazy things like "After school today, I think I'll take a bus into downtown to Bagley's Department Store and shop till after dark." She'd nod and say, "That's nice, Andi."

One day when she was out back hanging laundry on the clothesline, I climbed up on a kitchen chair, took the bottle down, and sniffed it. I couldn't understand how Grandmom could drink that stuff! It smelled like a mixture of mosquito repellant and the rubbing alcohol she poured on my insect bites when I forget to use the repellant. I knew better than to taste the stinky concoction; Grandmom had warned me that Geritol was strictly for adults.

So it had come down to this: I was condemned to spend my entire sixth-grade year in Mr. Banner's class, without prospect of parole. I sure wished there was a Geritol made for kids so that my mind could go on vacation too.

The shift in my attitude began the next day. Don't ask me why. I guess when all hope is squelched, other things take root, kind of like a cactus growing in the desert. Grandmom always said that a person could get used to hanging if they hung long enough. I was finding out, firsthand, that that was true.

Vanished were any hopes of returning to Alfreda and my beloved old chums (except for the boys, of course, who were all idiots like Jimmy Smithers). My despair had hardened to resignation. I had no other choice. I began observing my new classmates like cell mates, keeping my mind sharp and my eyes open.

By the second week, I had already found three things to be grateful for. The first one, oddly enough, was Bertha Riggs.

I easily could have deteriorated into Bertha's whipping board. If she wasn't pulling on my hair, she was whispering, "White girl! White girl!"—trying to fray my nerves and distract me from my lessons. My strategy had been to ignore her. And it worked. By that second Monday, she began using my actual name. No more yanks on my ponytail either. Sometimes during arithmetic, in an attempt to break her boredom, she even began braiding it. Her stinky fingers riffling through the strands of my hair felt soothing, like a back massage.

The next consolation prize was the discovery that we were going to have art class once a week beginning in October and that the new Ken doll, Mr. Alphonse, was going to be the instructor.

And the third condolence was the realization that Mr. Banner was not going to be a bad teacher after all. Though he was old, maybe forty or so, and set in his somber ways, exuberance rushed into his pale face the moment he cracked open our history book. He took teaching quite seriously, dressing the part of a college professor, complete with patches on the elbows of his tweed suit coats and hush puppy shoes. On his desk, he had a small picture of a woman who I presumed was his wife. She was plump, unsmiling like him, and had dark-rimmed glasses and short, fuzzy hair that looked as if she had left tiny rollers in overnight. At first glance, I thought she was his mother, but when I took my first spelling paper up to his desk and examined the photograph up close, I could see she wasn't as old as I had first thought—tired-looking, but not so old.

Mr. Banner wore a sadness that had congealed on his face as if he was accustomed to being crushed on a regular basis, not unlike Abraham Lincoln's gloomy expression in the portrait hanging on the wall near the door. Named in his honor, our school had a particular obligation to commemorate Lincoln, and studying his life was a traditional part of our sixth-grade curriculum. Because Castalia sat less than forty miles from the Illinois border, the sixth grade always culminated in the customary class outing to Lincoln's home in Springfield, Illinois—a day trip that took just a few hours longer in its entirety than the regular school day.

Devoting an entire year to Lincoln was fine with me. I was remaining vigilant in my prayers to be the next sixth grader to see Lincoln's ghost, and anything that might help me in that pursuit was well worth my undivided attention. It couldn't hurt to know as much about the man as possible. After all, if I was lucky enough to meet up with his ghost, I had to break the ice with some small talk and polite banter—you know, inquire about his sons and his wife, Mary Todd, before I blurted out my real questions about life after death.

The first project Mr. Banner had doled out was one researching the effects of the Civil War on our own state of Indiana. Studying history was a lot more fun, he said, if we could relate its relevance to our own lives. Mr. Banner was adept at weaving the threads between then and now, making each history lesson come alive. For the past few days, we had done our assigned reading, and now we were reviewing our lessons before the first big test.

"President Lincoln's initial call to put down the rebellion was for how many volunteers?" Mr. Banner scanned our faces for the answer, ready to call on anyone who did not break eye contact with him. "Howard?"

"75,000."

"That's correct. 75,000. And what was the number of soldiers required from Indiana?"

Howard responded again, even before he could be called upon: "7,500."

"Right again," Mr. Banner said. "But a lot more young men than that answered the call to fight. In fact, many thousands returned to their homes bitterly disappointed that they were not selected to serve. These disappointed young gentlemen thought they would never be called to fight because the war was expected to end quickly. Instead, the Civil War went on for how many years? . . . Andi?"

"Four," I said, and when Mr. Banner told me I was correct, Bertha congratulated me from behind with a proud shove on my shoulder.

"By the end of the Civil War," Mr. Banner continued, "more than 24,416 Hoosiers had been killed or had died, and more than twice that number returned to Indiana bearing disfiguring or debilitating wounds and scars."

My thoughts began to drift as I imagined maimed soldiers walking back home to Indiana, passing the rubble and devastation of war as they traveled by foot from state to state. I pictured Grandmom giving them a cup of coffee and a sandwich, the same way she feeds the hobos who stop by our porch during the summer. I imagined the soldiers staggering up to their own front porches and knocking on the door to let their families know they were home again. I imagined wives and mothers opening their doors, collapsing from joy at the sight of their maimed loved ones. My mind would wander then to what it would be like if the resurrected dead started rising from their graves, as some of my neighbors believed would happen at the end of time. They'd walk down the streets together after the cemeteries erupted, big bands of dead people dressed in their burial clothes, separating off one by one as they neared their own homes. I imagined hearing a knock at our front door, opening it, and seeing Mama and Daddy standing there; she'd still be wearing the silk silver dress and looking like a princess.

Our next assignment was to read about the Underground Railroad in our history book.

Bertha was hoarse-whispering, "Mule! Mule!" in an effort to rile up the mulatto boy, as Mr. Banner began distributing a mimeographed handout giving a first-person account of a traveling slave in Indiana. The purple ink was still fresh, slightly warping the paper with its dampness. I lifted it up to my nostrils and inhaled the proficient aroma of fresh mimeograph.

At recess, I found Alfreda.

"I got you a present," she said, "to cheer you up."

From the depths of her coat pocket, she yanked out a little package wrapped in Kleenex and presented it to me. Though the bubble gum they originally had come with had been chewed and spit out years ago, every single Beatles card in the stack featured a solo shot of George Harrison! No one knew better than I did that locating lone pictures of George—"the quiet Beatle" who was photographed the least—was not an easy accomplishment. It was just like Alfreda to be thoughtful enough to sort through dozens upon dozens of old Beatles cards (who knew where she even could've possibly found them), until she could assemble such a magnificent collection.

But it turned out it wasn't Alfreda's thoughtfulness as much as someone else's. "I got them at the bait shop," she said. "Ezra had tons of Beatles cards in the back room where he keeps the live bait, and he said he'd gather up all the pictures of George for me. You oughta come to the bait shop sometime, Andi. Ezra has a lot of cool things, though mostly it's just fishing stuff."

I had never met the man the colored kids called Ezra, but his name had become a bit of a legend around school. Sadly, I knew I'd never get to meet him firsthand because Ezra's Bait Shop was two blocks to the left of the school, in the midst of the colored neighborhood, and Grandmom would never allow such a trek. For the last few years, I'd been hearing about the bait shop and the magnificent candy counter where all the colored kids loaded up on special treats on their way to school each morning or on their way back to school after lunch—goodies like Sugar Daddies, Slow Poke suckers, wax lips, candy cigarettes, bubble gum cigars, Bit O' Honey, and Oke-Dokey Cheesy Popcorn that turned their fingers orange. Sometimes I'd give Alfreda a dime to buy for me the little gold bubble gum nuggets that came in a white pouch with yellow draw strings, my personal favorite.

I'd heard dozens of stories, mostly from Alfreda, about Ezra, the kind shop owner. Apparently, he had opened the bait shop, which used to be a dry goods store, a few years back. Alfreda said that he never minded that so many kids came into the shop at the same time just to buy candy. He always took time to talk to them, learn their names, listen to their stories—both him and his faithful German shepherd dog, Seth, who was always near Ezra's side. Seth seemed to listen to the kids' stories too, she said, his pointed ears always on alert as he calmly allowed dozens of sticky hands to ruffle up his coat and stroke his warm fur without so much as a snarl.

By the end of the third week of school, I was again despairing over my reassignment to the class from hell. Shunning my current classmates, I continued to hang around with Alfreda and my old chums on the playground. I could hardly wait for the recess bell to ring so that I could feel safe and normal again.

As they relayed their class experiences in Mr. Jackson's sixth grade, my heart would quietly break. Besides exacerbating an aching sense of loneliness, their stories were a solid measure of how much slower we were moving in Mr. Banner's class. They were already on the fourth chapter in their history books while we lingered painstakingly on the second, waiting for those kids who couldn't read very well to decipher the text during Oral Hour. Like salt on the wound, they shared their funny stories, too—how they would make silly faces at each other when

Mr. Jackson was writing on the blackboard and his back was turned. Innocent shenanigans.

They had no idea how mean the pranks were in Mr. Banner's class, if "pranks" was even the right word for them. Every day, somebody was making somebody cry, disfiguring a textbook, belting out a swear word, or talking at the same time Mr. Banner was trying to teach. He was forced to paddle one of the boys in our class nearly every day, instructing the bad-boy-of-the-moment to leave the room and wait for him in the boy's bathroom while he dug out the wooden paddle from his bottom desk drawer. Sometimes we actually could hear the pounding from our desks.

The first few weeks, the boys would usually return to the classroom with tears in their eyes. But not anymore. The more often Mr. Banner paddled them, the more resilient the stupid boys became, like a deadly virus. Sometimes they even laughed now when they returned to the classroom.

Without me to pick on—or the mulatto boy who flashed an obscene finger whenever she called him "Mule"—Bertha Riggs was focusing her attention on a new target: Keely, the new colored girl who wore her hair in a flip. If her hairdo wasn't enough fodder for Bertha's wrath, Keely chatted endlessly about her home life on the white side of Lincoln School. She was crazy about Mark Lindsay of Paul Revere and the Raiders and hated Motown. She would never dream of setting foot in the bait shop. Her father was a dentist with an office uptown, and she was excited about the prospect of getting braces.

Whenever Mr. Banner turned his back or was out paddling one of the boys, Bertha hurled dry paper balls at Keely, one after the next, until it looked like snow on the floor surrounding her desk. But by the end of the third week of school, they had escalated into pure spitballs, sealed tight with Bertha's cheesy Oke-Dokey saliva. Keely tried to ignore them at first, but the strategy didn't work for her. Now, Keely would whirl around and whimper, "Cut it out!"—her shaky voice belying her terror.

Showing fear was the worst thing she could do. The more rattled she became, the more delight Bertha derived from taunting her. "Keely's a big, 'fraidy baby," she'd hiss from across the room. "Don't start crying now. Go suck on your bottle."

The one thing that remained unchanged from last year was that I was still a patrol girl. Thank God for that. It was my one chance to escape from Mr. Banner's zoo and find some semblance of normalcy. At three o'clock every afternoon, I still was able to slip on my white patrol sash, as I'd done for the past three years, and receive my assignment to monitor the halls, or the stairs, wherever Mrs. Phillips put me that week. It gave me an odd peace to wander through the quiet hallways by myself, savoring the solitude before the bell rang at 3:10 p.m. on the dot, and the bedlam began.

During that last full week of October, Mrs. Phillips had assigned me to my favorite location of all: the top of the stairs leading to the auditorium/gymnasium. We never really knew which one to call it—auditorium or gymnasium—since it was one huge room that doubled as both. Mostly we used it as a gym, where we dribbled basketballs, practiced push-ups on gym mats, or exercised to the "Go, You Chicken Fat, Go!" song. When we needed it to be an auditorium, the janitor brought out a thin tarp to cover the shiny gymnasium floor and then arranged chairs in neat rows to face the wooden stage, usually obscured by a heavy purple velvet curtain. On both sides of the big room were two oddly shaped rooms, one that was used for storage and the other for band/orchestra practice.

I liked this patrol assignment the best because the only traffic was the trickle of kids coming out from band and orchestra practice. It was an easy, restful beat. Besides the small number of students at that location, they never needed patrolling. None of them ever ran down the steps or even walked too fast, mostly because they were weighed down with heavy instruments.

At about 3:20 p.m. on that last Friday in October, I was just about to pack it up for the day, when Howard Taylor, decked in his usual fastidious bow tie, began going the wrong way on the stairs, heading back up toward the gymnasium, not down toward the main floor. I reminded him that it was strictly forbidden to go back to the third floor after three o'clock, but Howard was persistent. It was an emergency, he explained. He had left his clarinet reeds by his band chair, and he was playing in a recital that weekend. The desperate look on his face was enough to melt the most resolved of patrol girls.

"Well," I said slowly, "if you insist, then I'll go back up with you."

Together, Howard and I climbed the staircase that led to the auditorium/gymnasium. We opened the heavy double doors and walked across the gym floor, and I followed him to the side room with the low vaulted ceiling that served as the band room. Standing by the oval door, I kept watch as Howard scanned the hardwood floor for his pack of clarinet reeds. "I sure appreciate this," he said, smiling at me, before reaching down to the floor and grabbing the little box.

It was then that we both heard noises—slow, distant, heavy footsteps, followed by a thud.

"What was that?" Howard's eyes widened. "Nobody's supposed to be up here after three o'clock."

I shrugged, trying to remain calm, but actually, I was terrified that one of the teachers had heard us and followed us upstairs. If that was true, Howard and I were both going to be in big trouble, especially me—I was a patrol girl, entrusted to enforce the school rules, not break them. I could see it now—I'd be kicked off the patrol squad, and then the whole school day (except recess) would be one never-ending, excruciating ordeal. Maybe I'd be sent down to Principal Mortenson's office. Maybe Mr. Banner would paddle me.

I pressed my finger up to my lips and motioned for Howard to come away quickly so that we could retreat back downstairs together and make a quick getaway before we were spotted. He nodded, intuiting my plan, and tiptoed toward me, clutching his little package of reeds.

As lightly as we could, we pushed through the door of the band room. Still tiptoeing, we moved into the dark gymnasium toward the staircase that would take us back down to the safety of the second floor. We had nearly made it to the exit when we suddenly heard another sound. This time, it was a muffled moan—half-animal, half-human—coming from just behind the velvet curtains on the auditorium stage.

"Mmmm, mmmmm, mmmm," the deep, low voice vibrated.

In stunned silence, Howard and I watched as the curtains began to move slightly, the big gold "L" embroidered at the very top wavering, as if a breeze was wafting through it.

"Mmmmm, ahhhh, ooo." It was unmistakably the wailing of a man.

I looked at Howard with raised eyebrows, my body frozen into a shrug, "Who on earth could be back there?" I whispered.

"It must be Lincoln's ghost!" he gasped, his eyes bulging.

Lincoln's ghost! My heart fluttered inside of me like a caged bird. Of course! Why hadn't I thought of that? All this time, I'd been praying for this very thing, and now I didn't recognize my own destiny looming in front of me. Who else could it possibly be?

"Let's get out of here!" he said.

But I shook my head and grabbed his sleeve so that he wouldn't escape. I was the one responsible for invoking Abraham Lincoln's spirit in the first place, and now I was resolved to see this thing through. "Be careful what you pray for," Grandmom always said. Now I knew what she meant.

My legs felt heavy, like in those dreams when they seem encased in cast iron. I loosened my grasp on Howard's shirt and forced myself to inch toward the velvet curtain, toward the strange mewling.

"Andi, don't!" Howard whispered from his spot by the exit.

But I knew my chance had arrived. In my mind, I was rehearsing. "Hello, Mr. Lincoln," I would greet him politely. "I hope that your wife, Mary Todd, is doing well." Slowly, I kept moving, pantomiming my words until I finally reached the three steps to the stage. I drew a deep breath as I mounted the first step, then the second, and finally, the third and last one. I was standing on the stage.

"Oooooo." The eerie moan came again, magnified by my proximity.

"Hey, Abraham Lincoln!" I shouted out, "Come out right now!" *So much for the polite banter*, I thought, stupidly.

The sound stopped.

I paused, stunned, my heart lifting like a rocket inside my chest. It really *must be* Lincoln's ghost behind that curtain! Otherwise, the real culprit would have emerged, madder than bejeezus, or hands in the air, surrendering. Summoning all the courage I could muster, I flung back the heavy velvet draping with one quick thrust of my trembling arm.

The backdrop curtain near the side exit was still fluttering as if someone had just rushed against it . . . but no one was there, and not one more sound could be heard.

Chapter 4

To this day, I feel responsible—sometimes in the form of guilt, sometimes vindication—for having a hand in manipulating John Malone's destiny, as if somehow, all my loneliness in Mr. Banner's class planted a seed somewhere in the cosmos that propelled John out of his world and into mine.

Like manna from the heavens, John simply appeared on that next Monday after the near sighting of Lincoln's ghost, which just happened to be Halloween Day. Nearly everyone in Mr. Jackson's class had donned colorful costumes. Alfreda came dressed like a cat, complete with pipe cleaner whiskers and erect velveteen ears. Only a few people in our class dressed up. The frail white girl with the cleft palette transformed herself into Snow White, resplendent in a sparkly, powder blue princess gown with fake white fur trim around the sleeves and hemline and a pretty mask covering her deformed face, probably the one day of the year when she could feel beautiful. One of the boys came dressed like the Pink Panther, and Keely wore a nurse's cape, hat, and white smock, borrowed from her father, the dentist.

As for me, I considered dressing up but decided against it. I didn't see the point. The way I figured it, wearing a costume was just one more way to potentially attract needless ridicule. Surviving in Mr. Banner's classroom required constant vigilance, and parading around in a silly costume only tempted the fates.

After our brush with Lincoln's ghost the Friday before, both Howard and I had sworn ourselves to secrecy, mostly because we thought we would get in big trouble if we made it known we were creeping around the auditorium after three o'clock. We even made a blood-brother pact about it, puncturing ourselves with a safety pin and mingling our blood together. But the temptation proved too great for either one of us. First thing Monday morning, he ratted to two of his best friends, and I spilled the beans to Alfreda. Before we knew it, both sixth-grade classes were buzzing with the knowledge that Abraham Lincoln's ghost was lurking one floor over our heads, ready to reveal himself to the next sixth grader at any given moment.

When the news finally reached Mr. Banner, he appeared shaken and angry and then amused. Trying to squelch our fears, he reassured us that ghosts simply did not exist. But when Howard and I were adamant that we had heard eerie sounds—human sounds for the most part—just behind the velvet curtains of the stage, he began to change his attitude. Not one student or one teacher had come forward to take credit or to provide any other explanation for the peculiar noises. Who else could it possibly have been? we beseeched him.

Finally, he waved his hand in resignation. "Well, maybe so," he said. "As a matter of fact, Abraham Lincoln had a number of supernatural experiences associated with him, some when he was living and many after his death. These supernatural tales happen to be part of his lore. And not just here at our school."

"Whatchu mean?" Bertha Riggs sat up in her chair. I think it was the first time all year that she had asked a question in class.

"Well," he said, pausing as if deciding whether to continue and then nodding to himself, "I suppose that it's all part of studying Abraham Lincoln. I guess it wouldn't hurt to talk a little about some of the mystical experiences surrounding our sixteenth President. They're really quite well documented by history."

As Mr. Banner walked over to the file cabinet behind his desk, the room got so quiet you could have heard Kathy O'Connor pull snot out of her nose, like she frequently did. But no one cared to catch her in the act this morning. All eyes were on Mr. Banner as he slowly opened the third file drawer and retrieved a fairly thick manila folder.

"Lincoln's ghost purportedly still haunts the White House," he continued as he sifted through the tome of papers. "And other places, too. In fact, the oldest actual haunting is connected to his tomb in Springfield."

Bernard Wilson's mouth dropped open slightly, and Robbie Taggert's too. It was nearly ten-thirty, about the time each morning that Robbie started getting restless and doing something contemptible enough to land him in the boys' bathroom, awaiting his next paddling. But not today.

"Let me read a poem to you, written by Vachel Lindsay," Mr. Banner said. "It's called 'Abraham Lincoln Walks at Midnight.' Perhaps some of you have even heard this poem before. Anyone?"

No one raised their hand or even nodded. Adjusting his glasses with a slight look of amusement, Mr. Banner began to read the poem:

> "It is portentous, and a thing of state;
> that here at midnight, in our little town;
> a mourning figure walks, and will not rest;
> near the old courthouse, pacing up and down . . ."

The classroom door swung open suddenly, the unexpected noise jarring our riveted attention. Principal Mortenson stepped into the room, accompanied by a boy whom none of us had ever seen before. His caramel-colored hair was cut into a Beatles haircut, much longer than the tidy crew cuts all the other boys were wearing. His head was tilted slightly downward, but his eyes were not downcast.

Principal Mortenson walked over to Mr. Banner, turning his back toward the class, and slipped him an index card as they exchanged some words that no one else could hear. Mr. Banner looked serious, nodding a few times to whatever the principal was saying to him. Then, Principal Mortenson turned around, smiling tersely at the new boy and obligatorily at the rest of us, and exited the room.

"Class," Mr. Banner said, "it appears that we have a new student joining our class. This is Johnny Malone."

"John," the new boy corrected, his voice soft but firm.

"Sorry—John Malone," Mr. Banner repeated. " . . . Anyway, it seems that John Malone has transferred over to us from St. Matthew's Catholic School. And . . . what else?" He scanned the index card he was holding for more information. "And he just turned twelve years old, two weeks ago. Is that right, John?"

He nodded.

"Is there anything else we should know about you?"

John indicated that there was nothing more to know by a quick shake of his head, his Beatles bangs moving just enough to reveal dark mahogany eyebrows.

Despite the gesture, we all surmised that there was a great deal more to the story. St. Matthew's was less than a mile away from Lincoln, and no one transferred to another school in the middle of the year, especially in the middle of their sixth-grade year, unless there was a mighty good reason—or a mighty bad reason, more likely. Though Mr. Banner was grinning at him, John Malone did not return the smile.

Mr. Banner pointed to an empty desk in the back row. "John, why don't you take that seat over there," he said.

With that, John Malone began his long descent down the aisle toward his awaiting desk, his head still bent downward, his eyes scanning our faces as he passed our unabashed stares, each of us scrutinizing the details of his face, his clothes, his movements. Besides the Beatles haircut, his eyes were the next thing I noticed. Something about his penetrating, guarded gaze reminded me of George Harrison—John Malone was bearing our gawking the same skeptical way that George Harrison handled pesky reporters who plied him with stupid questions. ("What do you call your haircut?" they had asked George; "Arthur," he replied.) John Malone looked as if he might be bottling a similar sarcastic comeback should any of us have the audacity to ask anything too personal.

"I bet they kicked him out of Catholic school 'cause of his hair," Bertha Riggs whispered in my ear, her voice loud enough for a few to hear.

"Class, please open your science books and silently read pages forty-five and forty-six while I gather up textbooks for John," Mr. Banner instructed, moving toward the back of the room where the extra books were stacked.

"Science?" Andrew Filipek whined, "but I thought you were gonna read us the poem about Lincoln's ghost."

"Abraham Lincoln's ghost will just have to hold its horses," Mr. Banner said. "And so will you, Andrew."

I tried to concentrate on page forty-five, but I couldn't even get through the first paragraph, despite several tries, without turning around to check on the newest addition to our class. At twelve years old, John Malone had the most perfect face I'd ever seen: George Harrison eyes, dark eyebrows, a perfect nose, and full lips. Not to mention that full head of shiny Beatles hair. And yet, maybe because of the tension I detected in him (already faint lines creased the skin beneath his eyes), it seemed his face might not be so perfect as he grew into it. It was like noticing the smallest of chinks, a fissure maybe, in a masterpiece work of art.

But right now, at this moment, John Malone's face was matchless, in its prime. It took every muscle I had to move my eyes toward my science book and away from him.

In one fell swoop, I was in love. My world, rearranged. All of a sudden, boys had evolved from objects of disdain to beings of curiosity, and all because one among them had risen like a beacon of mystery and intrigue.

Chapter 5

It's amazing the mannerisms you observe when you're stuck with the same people seven hours a day, five days a week. The thirty-one students who made up Mr. Banner's class totaled sixty-two eyes, meaning that every peccadillo imaginable was brought to scrutiny at one time or another. We learned that Mary Washington twisted and pulled out her own eyelashes; Roxanna Trixler's long index finger could usually be found twirling a strand of her strawberry-blonde hair into a tight rope; Denny Bingham's tongue slid out of the side of his mouth when he was lost in concentration; and Kathy O'Connor actually ate her own boogers!

As for John Malone, besides hardly ever smiling, he had a tendency to not move his head too much. Just his butterscotch-brown eyes moved—to the left or right, up or down—scanning the confines of Mr. Banner's classroom like a barbed wire fence he was plotting to scale.

Besides John, I had a lot of other things on my mind during that second week in November. I was miserable. Mr. Banner had gone and taken my clandestine, sacred prayer to meet up with Lincoln's ghost and diminished it to a classroom assignment. Rather than just *telling* us what he already knew about the supernatural occurrences surrounding Abraham Lincoln, Mr. Banner decided to challenge us—since we were so interested—to do the research ourselves.

Not wanting to take too much time on the subject, he decided to assign just four students to four different aspects of Lincoln's mystical folklore as part of our ongoing studies of Lincoln's life. He selected the students at random, but—as usual—my luck didn't allow me to be one of them, though John Malone was. Next, Mr. Banner had the four students draw folded pieces of paper, on which he had written the specific topics on the subject, from a glass bowl. Beginning next Tuesday, the first of the oral reports would begin.

The other kids were excited by the new, scary addition to our Lincoln curriculum, but not me. By making Lincoln's ghost a class project to which I had no personal contribution, Mr. Banner, albeit unknowingly, had stolen something private.

For some reason, maybe because John Malone's lack of attention was branding a hole inside my heart as deep as I'd ever felt, I was grieving for my parents all over again. Or maybe it was because Mr. Slaby had to put his old white poodle, Pom Pom, to sleep. Every morning on my way to school, I had to pass the fire hydrant where Pom Pom used to pee. I wondered where Pom Pom was now, or if he was anywhere at all. Pom Pom had lived on this earth more than fifteen years, even longer than me. I ached for the familiar sight of his old, watery eyes with the black stains underneath them. But beyond my sorrow was the inconsolable grief of poor old Mr. Slaby. Pom Pom had been his whole world, his reason to wake up in the morning. The sight of Mr. Slaby's anguished eyes shattered my heart.

Death was unfathomable to me in its cruelty. One day, Pom Pom was here, wearing his blue rhinestone collar, trudging to the fire hydrant to pee, and the next day, he was gone, vanished, his blue collar empty. I just couldn't absorb the mercilessness of that reality. Was Pom Pom somewhere far away waiting for Mr. Slaby to join him, or was he just rotting away—like Mr. Baxter believed—in the tiny grave Mr. Slaby had dug for him in his backyard? I was newly desperate—frantic, really—to learn the truth about death. Some nights, the pain inside of me was so intense that it actually hurt, like a stomachache, only higher, nearer to my heart, and I'd feel like I was going crazy. I couldn't even talk to Grandmom; she was on her Geritol again.

My loneliness was unbearable.

It was about that time when big Bernard Wilson stood on the back steps of the school and proclaimed to us on the playground that saying the words "colored" and "Negro" was disrespectful and no longer appropriate. He said the new term to use was "black." He said that Ezra at the bait shop had told him so.

I wasn't sure if Bernard was right or not, even though I made a point of promising him that I would call him "black" should the occasion to describe him ever come up. But inside, I had my doubts. If "black" really was the correct term, I wondered why President Johnson was still saying the word Negroes (he always pronounced it "nig-ruhs") in the speeches he made on television. Besides that, I wasn't certain that the new word described Negroes any better than the word "white" described Caucasians.

One time at recess the year before, a whole bunch of us girls had put our hands together to see how different our skin tones were. Carol Miller's skin was the color of porcelain, with thin blue veins shining through it; my skin was kind of rose-tinted; Marcia Harper's had an olive cast to it; Alfreda's skin was the color of milk chocolate; Jackie Scuggins's skin was the color of a root beer float; and on and on it went. When it came right down to it, none of us were either black or white, but a whole spectrum of colors in between.

Bernard took a deep breath after his proclamation, as if he was proud of himself for saying something important. He even looked smarter, his eyes full of life and purpose, his back straighter, as if—to him—calling himself "black" gave him a whole new appreciation for who he was. Maybe it was kind of like being called "Andi" was for me. I hated the name Andrea. To me, it was a name that conjured up the image of a spoiled brat, dressed in white tights, puffy velveteen dress, and long Shirley Temple locks.

In Bernard's case, it seemed something far more important than that, since it was describing a whole race of human beings, not just one inconsequential name. For the very first time, Bernard Wilson seemed to like himself.

That was good enough for me. Right then and there, I swore to myself that I'd never say the words "colored" and "Negro" again.

Mr. Alphonse, the cute Ken-doll art teacher, turned out to be a real oddball, a nonconformist in every way, the total opposite of the staid, intellectual Mr. Banner. It was not unusual for Mr. Alphonse to leap on top of the desktops in the middle of class, skipping from desk to desk like a giant, well-groomed grasshopper, ranting about the great artists—Monet, Picasso, Leonardo da Vinci—daring us to, one day, aspire to their league. "It all begins now!" he would shout. "Feel your dreams! Feel your soul! Feel your art!"

Then, he would jump down from the desks and make it personal. He once grabbed Howard by the tips of his bow tie, swirling each end between his fingers and imploring, "You, Mr. Taylor? Are you the next Leonardo da Vinci just waiting to burst out of your shell?"

Discipline was never a problem in art class, like it was in music class with old Mrs. Henderson, because everyone truly believed that Mr. Alphonse was too passionate to provoke. Who knew what he might do if someone pushed him too far—make them leap across the desktops along with him? Make them write a research paper on the life of Picasso? Besides, his bizarre antics were entertaining enough without any help from the rest of us. Only tough Robbie Taggert was driven one day to desperation by Mr. Alphonse's unconventional teaching methods. Running his fingers through his carrot-colored hair, Robbie muttered under his breath, "That guy's a psycho."

When Mr. Alphonse asked him to repeat what he had said, this time loud enough for the entire class to hear, we held our breath. "Well?" Mr. Alphonse had persisted.

Robbie dissolved into low chuckles and replied, "I didn't say anything out loud that everyone doesn't already know."

"Well then, what a ridiculous waste of your time and ours!" Mr. Alphonse said, his smile gleaming. "If everyone already knows something, what's the point in repeating it out loud? Our job in this class is to be original! To express our individuality and set ourselves apart! I suggest the next time you say something out loud, make it something that no one knows or has ever dreamed of."

Bertha Riggs, too, was distracted from her usual game in the presence of Mr. Alphonse. Art class was the only time of the week that she eased up on her incessant torment of Keely Summers. Back in Mr. Banner's class, she had now escalated to calling Keely obscene names and threatening to beat her up. "Keely is a shit box! Keely is a shit box!" she would hoarse-whisper across the room when Mr. Banner was too busy to hear. But in art class, Bertha didn't utter a peep.

Mr. Alphonse was a sharp dresser, and his golden hair was shiny and wavy, with a big pompadour that shook whenever he moved his head. This was his first teaching job. I thought that maybe he acted so wild because he wasn't married yet. A wife certainly would not allow him to behave like such a lunatic. During recess, Alfreda and I had tried to match him up with Miss Burden, the first-grade teacher, touting each of their virtues to the other one and even devising a plan to get them to stand together on the playground to watch us play a rollicking game of Bounce a Fly. Once they were side by side, we gently pushed them together, as if it was an accident, her arm brushing against his chest in the process. They both turned beet red and didn't look each other in the eyes, so we eventually dropped our scheme.

Music class was a completely different story. Mrs. Henderson was an old lady, a few years away from retirement, with curly salt and pepper hair and dark-rimmed eyeglasses, and she was profoundly over-perfumed. Two times a week, we visited the music room, where she planted herself behind an old upright piano, distributing her bifocaled gaze equally between the sheet music and us, as she coaxed us to sing songs from our ancient music books about scarlet ribbons and syncopated clocks or old standbys like the Mexican Hat Dance.

Most of the kids in Mr. Banner's class were just not the type to warble sweet songs on command. The situation had escalated to the point where the boys, including John, were refusing to cooperate with her at all. If there was any singing to be done, it was up to us girls, and we did it as much to irritate the boys as to indulge poor Mrs. Henderson.

That Thursday afternoon, the second week in November, finally drove Mrs. Henderson to the point of no return, unraveling her in front of us like a ball of yarn. The trouble all started after she tried to force the boys to sing about scarlet ribbons again, and Robbie flashed her an obscene finger. She told him to go to the rear of the classroom and stand in the corner, and he told her to go to hell. That retort sent most of the boys, and Bertha Riggs, into fits of hysteria. The more she tried to shush them, the louder the waves of laughter became, until nearly the entire class was howling, except for a few of us who weren't certain just what to do.

Mrs. Henderson's bottom lip quivered for nearly a full minute before she began to cry. Not a little sniffle either, but hard, gut-wrenching sobs that distorted her face and convulsed her body, her mascara spreading across her cheeks like black tar. I wanted to rush to the piano bench and comfort her, but I was afraid. Finally, she stood up, fled from the classroom, and never looked back.

And that brings us to the following Monday. Mr. Banner informed us that Mrs. Henderson had decided to take an early retirement and would not be returning to Lincoln Elementary School ever again. Robbie giggled when he heard the news. I had a sick feeling in my stomach.

"So, why don't you just go to the bait shop after school with Alfreda?" Keely Summers whispered to me that Monday afternoon, the same day we found out about Mrs. Henderson. She knew it was a shocking suggestion to make.

I smiled at her, intrigued by the prospect. Two weeks earlier, I would have replied, "Are you nuts? You know I can't go to the bait shop." Keely understood the unstated reason as well as I did. Ezra's Bait Shop was strictly off limits simply because of its location, and that was a rule that all the white kids at Lincoln Elementary School had obeyed for as many years as I could remember.

So what had changed it? John Malone had changed it, that's what. In just two weeks at our school, John had taken it upon himself to shake up decades of history. He regularly patronized the bait shop right along with the black kids, stuffing his pockets with gum and candy without giving it a second thought. Sometimes he and Lamar or Bernard would exchange Pez for suckers or Sugar Daddies for spearmint gum, the three of them dealing their candy stashes on the playground to strike the best jackpot, like seasoned old poker players.

"But what would you tell your grandmother?" Keely asked.

I shrugged. Dawdling after school had never been much of an issue unless I came home really, really late—like after five o'clock. Grandmom had her set routines. She liked to watch soap operas all afternoon and then settle in for a long, uninterrupted nap—her beauty sleep, she called it. Her habit was to wake up close to five o'clock and then start cooking our dinner, which we usually ate around seven o'clock. The only time she deviated from this schedule was when she played bingo with the Catholic ladies at St. Matthew's on Friday nights. After bingo, sometimes, they'd play a game or two of rummy. Grandmom swore the old ladies cheated, but she enjoyed herself just the same.

Keely had become my second best friend. Since I needed a good friend in Mr. Banner's class, and so did she, we kind of bonded together in our loneliness, at first out of necessity. The friendship ignited the first time we sat together in art class, and we tried to suppress our giggles over Mr. Alphonse's antics. The more we tried to suppress our laughter, the more we couldn't control it. But he didn't get mad. In fact, he winked at us and then made a silly face—crossing his eyes and flapping his tongue—to make us giggle even more. Mr. Alphonse seemed to take a special interest in Keely, mostly because her paintings turned out so out much better than the rest of our efforts.

One by one, the desks in Mr. Banner's class were reassembled from the original alphabetical arrangement into an order that made more sense to Mr. Banner in terms of nipping discipline problems in the bud and accessibility to the paddle. By serendipitous coincidence, Keely and I had been reshuffled right next to each other in the back of the room a few weeks ago, which was a fine arrangement from both our perspectives. I now sat in the last desk in the first row—three large windows and the fire escape exit door on my left—with Keely beside me in the next row on my right. Except for a seat beside John Malone, it was the best spot in the room.

From my new desk, I had the opportunity to stare outside the windows when my attention waned, losing myself in daydreams, mesmerized by the gold and russet leaves on the numerous old oak trees as they slowly drifted to the ground. Besides that, from my vantage point in the back of the room, I could gaze to my heart's content at John Malone, who sat one seat ahead of Keely in the row to her right, without anyone catching on.

I actually considered Keely's suggestion about visiting the bait shop for a long time that afternoon. Alfreda already knew I liked John, and now Keely was the second person to learn my secret. Both sympathized with my plight, especially since everyone knew that Cathy Gordon and Roxanna Trixler both liked John Malone too. Roxanna was the prettiest girl in our class—dumber than a box of chalk but pretty enough to make her intelligence irrelevant. She had long, straight (almost like she ironed it, and maybe she did) strawberry-blonde hair that she twirled mindlessly with her index finger, her ocean blue eyes batting toward John half a million times a day. And Cathy, well, she had flunked sixth grade last year, so she had a year's jump on the rest of us in terms of body development and hormones. She looked like a full-fledged teenager in her cardigan sweaters and miniskirts. How could he resist either one?

They never said it out loud, but I knew what they were thinking. Neither Keely nor Alfreda (nor I, for that matter) believed I stood one iota of a chance of ever attracting John Malone's attention. The day after he appeared in class, I had decided to take out my ponytail and was now wearing my shaggy brown hair long and free. But it was bushy in all the wrong places, making my face look smaller and my nose look bigger. Grandmom told me I looked like I stuck my finger in the toaster.

"Think about it," Keely whispered again.

She was perceptive and had guessed that I liked John even before I told her so. ("How did you know?" I wondered, and she replied, "'Cause your eyes sparkle whenever you look at him.")

Keely got A's in nearly every subject we had, including reading, English, library, history and geography, music, art, science, spelling, writing, and arithmetic. The only C she got was in gym class, since she couldn't hand-walk the suspended, horizontal ladder or sink a basket to save her life. Her greatest wish was to become a doctor—either that or an astronaut, but it would be tough, she said, for a woman to become one of the few selected by NASA.

I wanted to persuade her to come to the bait shop with me, but I kept my mouth shut. Even though she was black, she would never consider the mission. Venturing into the black neighborhood would put her at risk of running into Bertha Riggs outside of the safety of the school grounds.

If Bertha Riggs was right about anything, she was right in her assessment that Keely seemed more like a white girl than a black girl. Keely even hated James Brown's new song, "I Got You (I Feel Good)," because she thought he squealed like a stuck pig. But what did it matter? Acting white didn't make her a bad person.

Keely continued to coax. "It's your only chance to talk to John."

She was right, of course, and I knew it. Class offered few opportunities to fraternize with John Malone. And neither did recess, where the boys played basketball together on one end of the playground, and the girls played Bounce a Fly or Four Square on the other. *That* was a sacred division that even John Malone wouldn't dare traverse.

Only my fear was holding me back from going to the bait shop, and it got me to thinking about what a crippling emotion it really was.

Take poor Mrs. Henderson, for example. She had dedicated her entire life to being a music teacher. Then, right as her long career neared its end, she had allowed her fear of Robbie Taggert and those other boys to get the best of her, sacrificing her lifelong passion under the strain of the humiliation they caused her. And Keely was afraid too. I kept urging her to try to brush off Bertha's taunting by acting like it didn't bother her in the least, but she couldn't pull it off. Every day, I watched her world grow smaller and smaller as she plotted how to avoid Bertha Riggs at every turn. Keely had the brains to become one of NASA's chosen few, I had no doubt. But I couldn't imagine her conquering the universe if she couldn't even venture to the other side of Lincoln Elementary School.

All because of fear.

Fear was a horrible, toxic thing. Maybe that was the lesson I was supposed to learn by being dumped in Mr. Banner's class. Fear was a monster that gathered deadly momentum if left unchecked. Fear, like a solar eclipse, was powerful enough to blot out every shred of light.

That's when I finally made the decision. The following day, Tuesday, I was going to conquer my own stupid fears, once and for all, and venture inside Ezra's Bait Shop. Tomorrow, I would look John Malone straight in his ginger-brown eyes and strike up a conversation.

Now all I had to figure out was what the heck I could possibly say to him.

Chapter 6

Mr. Banner sat behind his desk, uncharacteristically tapping his pencil in a jovial way that reminded me of Johnny Carson just after the commercial breaks. Of late, Mr. Banner had really changed. Gone was that serious, defeated expression, and in its place was a kind of quirky smile; one end of his mouth was much higher than the other, as if smiling was a new experience that his mouth hadn't yet mastered.

Flashing his crooked smile, Mr. Banner appeared almost as excited as we were to hear the first oral report about Abraham Lincoln and the supernatural. Carol Miller was the one to present it. Being the first one to do anything was a daunting obligation, but Carol stepped up in front of the class without one trace of nervousness. Pushing her glasses close up against the bridge of her nose, she gave a last-minute scan of the piece of notebook paper she was holding.

"My report," she began, "is about Abraham Lincoln's very first documented psychic experience. It happened when he was first elected president of the United States back in 1860, over one hundred years ago. At that time, he still lived with his family in Springfield, Illinois." She glanced at Mr. Banner to assure that he was pleased with her report thus far. He was and nodded at her. "By midnight on Election Day, he knew that he would be the next President," Carol continued. "After a whole night of celebration and parties, Abraham Lincoln returned to his home in Springfield early in the morning, and he went into his bedroom to rest because he was completely exhausted. In his bedroom, he had a large bureau with a big mirror on it.

"When Abraham Lincoln looked into the mirror, he saw a vision of himself. But it was not just a normal reflection of his face. What Lincoln saw were two separate and distinct images of his own face. One of the faces was slightly higher than the other and about five shades more pale—as white as a ghost. The vision disappeared and then reappeared a few minutes later. Lincoln said he was a little bothered by it, but not a whole lot.

"But when he told his wife, Mary Lincoln, about what he saw, she was scared. She thought it was a very bad omen. She said that the two faces meant that he would serve two terms in office. The one face was his real face, she said, meaning he would serve one full term in office. But the paleness of the second face meant he would be killed during the second term—which, of course, he was. President Lincoln was shot by John Wilkes Booth on Good Friday, April 14, 1865. He died the next day."

Carol's eyes then left her paper for the first time since she had looked at Mr. Banner. This time, she looked at us, pleased that she had been able to capture our undivided attention for the duration of her presentation. "And that's the end of my report," she announced.

Mr. Banner stood up from his desk and nodded again. "Very good, Carol," he said. "That was an excellent, very thorough essay. Do any of you have questions or comments for Carol?"

Robbie Taggert raised his hand. "I know what gave Lincoln the double vision."

"You do?" Mr. Banner raised his eyebrows.

"Sure," Robbie said. "If he was out partying all night, I think he was drunk when he got home. That's what gave him double vision. That's what my dad says happens to him when he's drunk."

"Well," Mr. Banner replied slowly, "I suppose it's a possibility. Anything is possible, although it wasn't in Mr. Lincoln's character to imbibe. Besides, drunk or sober, how do you account for Mrs. Lincoln's accurate interpretation of his vision?"

No one, not even Howard Taylor, had an explanation for that one.

My moment of truth had arrived. The first step I took in the opposite direction—toward the black neighborhood—was the hardest one. Alfreda remained by my side to lend moral support and to remind me why I was doing this crazy thing. Before I knew it, I was lost in a herd of black kids heading home from school, some of them ahead of us, some behind us, all walking in the same direction, toward Ezra's Bait Shop.

I walked with a little more bravado and certainty with every step I took. What I was doing felt natural, yet significant and daring, as if I was shedding something heavy that needed to be discarded, like a bulky sweater on a sweltering summer day. I wondered why something so silly as walking in the opposite direction of the school had remained such a big deal for all these years, why an imaginary boundary line had been drawn in the first place.

Once we reached the actual shop, all my fears returned. Alfreda held the door open for me and smiled. I paused and took a deep breath before I stepped inside.

Ezra's Bait Shop was a tiny store, consisting of four short aisles stacked neatly but densely with fishing poles, bait and tackle, and an array of strange-looking items (their purpose eluding me) hanging on long peg boards lining each walkway. In the back of the shop was a small section for fishing hats and a few waterproof vests. The live bait was kept in a separate room with a closed door and marked by a sign as being off-limits to students, unless accompanied by an adult. Here was where tanks of minnows, night crawlers, crawdads, leeches, and other worms were kept. (I knew this only because Alfreda had once visited the back room with her uncle, and she told me so.) Parallel to the front door, on the right, stood the cash register on a long wooden checkout counter, complete with a built-in glass showcase packed with assorted candy, snacks, and gum, the variety surpassing even the dime store's ample selection.

And behind this magnificent candy counter sat Ezra, the owner, on a tall, backless stool. He was not at all what I expected him to look like. What I expected to find was a scrappy old black man, ravaged around the edges by time and hard-earned wisdom. What Ezra was, in fact, was a slight, lean, young black man, probably in his late twenties, with a warm smile and a beautiful set of teeth—straight, clean, and pure white—against his light mocha skin. His black hair was long, reaching down to the small of his back, tied in braids that were too loose to be considered cornrows, too tight to be dread locks. His eyes were light, olive-colored, the color of split pea soup. But then, when he turned his head away from the window, they became topaz. When he turned his head back toward the light, they were olive again.

Ezra was magical, a stunning man. It was difficult not to keep staring at him. There was just no way, in one casual glance, to absorb all the unorthodox details that composed him.

Beside him on the hardwood floor sat his trusty German shepherd dog, Seth, his ears erect, his black eyes keen on scrutinizing each visitor who crossed the threshold of their shop, announced by tin bells that hung on the handle of the door. Seth, like his master, was a beautiful mixture of tans and browns and blacks.

Something easy and picturesque just flowed about the two of them, Ezra and Seth, as if they were a part of a natural landscape. I couldn't describe it, really; it was just a feeling, a vibration they gave off. But the moment I stepped foot inside the bait shop, all my tension about coming in the first place evaporated. I felt warmed and welcome.

"Greetings," Ezra said, smiling at me with his beautiful teeth. He flashed me a peace sign with slim, black fingers.

My fascination with Ezra was abruptly diverted by the sight of John Malone entering the bait shop; the bells on the doorknob clanged, and my heart accelerated. John looked right at me, maybe surprised to see a white girl in the bait shop, but maybe not. I wanted to say hi to him, but my voice had disappeared somewhere deep inside my throat, irretrievable.

Bernard Wilson followed close behind him. I guessed that if John had made a best friend at Lincoln, the honor would probably belong to Bernard, although John was still pretty much a loner.

"Take a picture, and it'll last longer," Bernard said, mocking my adoring gaze toward John.

I felt my face swell hot, probably the color of crimson red. I turned away.

Alfreda came to my rescue. "Shut up, Bernard!" she scolded. "Act your age, not your shoe size! Although with your big old feet, you probably will *never* act that old! This is Andi's first time in the bait shop, and you shouldn't be so nasty to her."

"First time?" Ezra said, smiling from behind the counter. "Oh, you know what we do for first-timers, don't you?" He slid the doors open from his side of the glass candy showcase, reached in, and pulled out four Slow-Poke suckers. "Here," he said, handing them to me, "First-time customers get to treat their friends to free candy."

I could hardly believe my good luck. Here I was, finally inside the bait shop, getting free suckers and being able to hand them over, one by one, to the outstretched hands of Alfreda, Bernard, and—John Malone. The moment seemed to be happening in slow motion, as John reached toward me to snatch the Slow Poke from my fingers. And then—he smiled at me!

It was a glorious moment. But I stoked it too long. Stuck, mired in my own immobility, I just stood there like a dope—my voice mute, my tongue thick, my lips too numb to smile back at him, leaving John no other choice than to roll his eyes and walk away.

"Man, that girl can't even talk, she's so ga ga over you!" Bernard said, doubling over with laughter. John laughed too.

My sacred moment had imploded. If it weren't for Ezra, I might have curled up into a ball and thrown myself into the Castalia River that very night. He stepped around from the other side of the counter and pressed his fingers tightly against my shoulder, partly in comfort, partly to rouse me from my stupor. "Tell you what," he said, "how 'bout you help me close out my cash register this afternoon? I could really use a helper today. You think that would be okay with your parents?"

"They're both dead," I said.

Ezra nodded, his eyes clouding. "I see."

"But my Grandmom wouldn't mind."

"You sure about that?"

I nodded. It was a half-truth. She never minded if I came home late. But she'd have a real conniption if she knew I'd been at the bait shop.

By that time, John and Bernard had moved to the back of the shop and were trying on the fishing hats. Alfreda was following close behind Bernard, giving him grief about some remark he had made to one of her neighbors earlier in the day. I knew she kind of liked him. Why couldn't I be more like Alfreda, I wondered, cool enough to smart off to the boy she liked? Not a moonstruck dummy like me.

A few more kids came into the bait shop, bidding Ezra to open up his candy showcase and then pointing on the glass and smudging it with their dirty hands as they chose their desired candy. I sat down on the floor beside Seth and stroked his soft, thick fur, waiting for further instruction on how to assist Ezra. I couldn't see John from my vantage point on the floor, but I could hear him and Bernard—and Alfreda—laughing together as they tried the fishing hats on each other in the back of the shop.

Eventually, the kids trailed out of the store, one by one. John and Bernard punched each other as they passed by me on the floor on their way to the door, joking together and trading "your mama . . ." insults as they swirled their Slow Pokes, compliments of me, across their tongues, without even a thank you for bestowing the free treats.

Alfreda squatted down beside me on the floor for a few seconds, tweaking Seth's ears. "You gonna be okay?" she asked.

I nodded dismally.

"Weeeell," she said, drawing out the word as if she was scrambling to come up with something positive to rouse my spirits, "at least he knows you like him now."

It was the worst thing she could have said. I feigned a sickly smile.

After Alfreda left, Ezra asked me to turn the sign around on the door so that it read "gone fishing" from the outside, rather than "open." It was four o'clock in the afternoon, his usual closing time.

Ezra brought out a huge metal tray filled with coins of all kinds and a cardboard box of flat paper coin rolls, along with another stool for me so that I could sit beside him at the counter. "Here's what I need you to do," he instructed. "Take the coins from this tray, sort them out by denomination, and start rolling them up in the appropriate coin rolls."

I nodded. He let me work on that project for a long time. I was already finished wrapping the nickels before he even tried to start up a conversation.

"You're a smart girl," he said finally. "What'd you say your name was again?"

"Andi. That's short for Andrea."

"Andi what?"

"Andi Powell."

Ezra stuck out his hand and flashed his perfect teeth. "Well, pleased to know you, Andi Powell. My name is Ezra Zachariah Thompkins."

I assumed he was just trying to be nice because he felt sorry for me. But I was glad for the distraction anyway.

"You like that boy, don't you?" he said, out the blue.

I shrugged and then surrendered the feeble fight and nodded. "I know he's out of my league," I said, fighting back silly tears as I began working on the dimes, shoving them into the money roll.

"Now, why you say that?" Ezra asked.

"'Cause there's just nothing special about me," I said. "I'm not the prettiest like Roxanna Trixler or the sexiest like Cathy Gordon or the smartest like Keely or the coolest like Alfreda. I want to be an 'est' at something too! Otherwise, what good am I?"

Ezra acted like he was concentrating on his receipts—he even pulled out some half-glasses so that he could see the light purple ink better—but he was listening pretty good too. "Tell you what," he said. "The way I see it is, you already *are* an 'est.' You're the best Andi Powell there is and ever will be. That makes you something special."

Big honor, I thought. Who would even *want* to be another Andi Powell?

Ezra sensed I wasn't buying it. "Why you think God made so many people?" he asked.

I shrugged once more.

"If only a few of us were born to be special, why would he go to all that trouble and make so many millions of other people? And why do you think every one of those people has to be different from the next one?"

I was stumped for an answer.

"Well, I'll tell you what I think," he said. "I think we all have a reason to be here, a special mission just for us and us alone to accomplish. No one else can do it. So though you ain't askin' for it, I'll give you my two cents." He leaned over and grabbed two pennies from the stack I had separated out and handed them to me. "When you're content with who you are, that's when you're an 'est'—at your prettiest, smartest, coolest, you name it. Just be yourself, and you'll have that boy talkin' to you in no time."

I looked up into Ezra's eyes, olive again. "You really think so?"

"I know so," he said.

The weight of the world seemed to lift from my shoulders as I began shoving some quarters inside the coin rolls.

"You gotta listen to your gut," Ezra said. "Dickens said that kids are 'fresh from God,' and you know what? I think he was right. You're closer to the angels when you're young, so pay attention to the things that move you now . . . Do you love that boy enough to break your heart?"

I looked up from my work, silent.

"Well, do you?"

"He kind of broke it already," I said.

Ezra smiled. "That's good! That's good! Isn't that good, Seth?" He scratched his fingers behind the dog's neck, and Seth's tail began beating against the counter in ecstatic agreement. "That's the only way that he can enter your heart—if it's broken. You dig? You got to till the ground deep enough if you want to plant something. You remember that."

I didn't really understand what Ezra was saying to me, but the part I could understand felt good; I felt comforted and hopeful. Being beside Ezra gave me a feeling like I never had before. It was like sailing into a safe harbor. Once again, I gazed up into his eyes, now amber in the late afternoon light. I had the feeling that his eyes were like magic pastures that went on and on, that I could climb into them, and never, ever want to come back out again.

Chapter 7

Mrs. Diggins was not about to let us demolish her in the same fashion we had destroyed poor Mrs. Henderson. In the first place, Mrs. Diggins was livid that she had been assigned to be the new music teacher in addition to her responsibilities as the morning kindergarten teacher. "Just because I don't teach a class in the afternoon doesn't mean I don't have more than enough to do already," she snarled to us the first day of music class.

Mrs. Diggins was a large, black woman, with gargantuan hips and gigantic breasts. Her blouses always bulged between the buttons, gaping apart and sometimes even coming undone, so she was constantly checking them with her long fingernails to ensure they were intact. When she wasn't policing her buttons, her usual stance was both hands pressed tightly against her hips, her eyes scanning the class, back and forth, like a sniper.

She really let us have it her first day as our music teacher. "Don't you all think for one minute that you can mess with me!" she warned. "I know all about the mean tricks you pulled with Mrs. Henderson, and I will *not*—repeat *not*—allow you to treat me with anything but respect. You all hear that? You even *think* about giving me any trouble, and I'll show you what trouble really means."

When Robbie let out a snicker, Mrs. Diggins walked over to him and whacked him across his cheek with the back of her hand, a smack so hard that it reverberated throughout the room. Robbie's check remained beet red for the next five minutes.

By the end of our first session with Mrs. Diggins, even Robbie was crooning about scarlet ribbons.

Tuesday afternoon had finally rolled around again, and it was Keely's turn to deliver the next oral report. Unlike Carol Miller, Keely was a bundle of nerves. Throughout the morning, she had pulled at the ends of her flip hairdo until some of the strands were stick-straight. I kept telling her not to worry because everything she did was outstanding, and I was confident that her oral report would not be an exception.

But when the time finally came for her to approach the head of the class, she was nearly paralyzed with anxiety. She had to begin her report three times over because her voice was trembling. Finally, after some reassurance and gentle coaxing from Mr. Banner, including a firm threat to Bertha Riggs that she would be paddled on the spot if she insisted on laughing, Keely was able to continue.

"M-my my re-report," she staggered on the third try, "is about how Abraham Lincoln got to be such a—such a—sad man."

She looked up at me because Mr. Banner said we would be graded on how well we made eye contact with the class in addition to the quality of our report. I smiled at her and nodded.

"Knowing about how h-hard his life was," Keely continued, "will make some of his supernatural experiences more understandable to us."

Mr. Banner nodded. "That's an excellent concept for your report, Keely. Well done!"

"From the beginning, he was born into a very poor family, and life was very hard. His mother died when he was still a child . . ."

My mind started to wander when Keely read that line from her report because I couldn't help but think about my own parents. I wondered if I was destined to be sad all my life, just like Lincoln. Before I knew it, I was mooning out the window again, staring at the last few leaves on the old oak trees that had not yet fallen off from their skeletal branches. It was that ugly time of late fall, when the remaining leaves had long lost their colors and were left behind, dry and brittle.

Thanksgiving Day was this Thursday, which meant a four-day weekend. Grandmom was already thawing out the frozen turkey in our refrigerator. I hated Thanksgiving, and all the holidays, mostly because they reminded me of how lonely we were—just me and Grandmom and two empty chairs at the dinner table.

" . . . All of these things combined to make him a serious man," Keely was saying when my attention finally returned to her report. I could see her confidence building. She was even starting to use expression as she read her report, which added enough punch to maintain my attention. "The Civil War, of course, caused him more great sorrow. He seemed to take the deaths on both sides as a personal loss, and his face got very old and lined while he was the president. He did not sleep well all those years he was in the White House, and his only source of joy and comfort were his two youngest sons, Willie and Tad.

"But then, in 1862, Willie died in the White House at the age of eleven of typhoid fever or some type of infection. This was a terrible blow to President Lincoln. Some said it was the worst tragedy of his life. Willie's funeral was held in the White House, and he was supposed to have been buried back in Springfield, Illinois, but Abraham Lincoln could not bear to have his son's body taken so far away from him. And so Willie's body was to be kept in a tomb in Washington that belonged to one of Lincoln's friends until Lincoln was no longer the president and they could return Willie's body to Springfield.

"Willie's tomb was located in a remote area of the cemetery in Washington that was built into the side of a hill. Lincoln could not get over the death of his son, and he grieved deeply. He even went to the cemetery during the night a couple of times and opened up the coffin to look at Willie again."

My mouth flew open when Keely read that line of her report, and Carol Miller actually gasped out loud. "Eeech!" yelped Robbie Taggert.

Pleased with the impact she was making, Keely ended her report with a dramatic flair, her confidence in full bloom. "Some say President Lincoln never did get over his beloved son's death. Mrs. Lincoln, too, was so grief-stricken that she even had some séances in the White House to try to contact Willie. There was a rumor that a grand piano in the White House levitated during one of these séances in 1863."

Several arms shot up with a sudden question. One of them belonged to Nancy, the girl with the cleft palette, and Keely called on her first. "What does levitate mean?"

Keely smiled, proud that she knew the answer. "It means it floated in the air."

The next day at recess, the boys were being jerks and trying to scare the girls. Robbie Taggert kept claiming stupid things like Willie's ghost was living in the basement in the boiler room next to the milk machine.

When we tried to walk away from them, they chased us and started singing that creepy song—"When you see a hearse go by, that's the sign that you're gonna die, the worms crawl in, the worms crawl out, the worms play pinochle on your snout . . ."

When recess was over, Carol Miller marched straight to Mr. Banner to lodge an official complaint.

"In music class, you can't get them to sing," Mr. Banner sighed under his breath, "and on the playground, they won't stop singing."

Because none of the boys would admit which ones were involved and which ones weren't, every single boy got a paddling that afternoon, even John Malone.

The next day, we had music class. "Okay, you little hooligans," Mrs. Diggins said, fighting a half-smile that was forming on her scarlet-painted lips. "Today, we're gonna sing some songs to uplift your sorry little souls during this season of Thanksgiving. We also need to start practicing for our Christmas program, but I think we'll hold off until next week on that."

With that, she whipped out a stack of papers where she had mimeographed lyrics from two verses of an old African American spiritual titled "Let Us Break Bread Together." After we inhaled the irresistible scent of fresh mimeograph, we settled down to business. I actually remembered hearing the hymn once on television, on the Saturday night after President Kennedy had been assassinated. A full choir was singing it, and Grandmom had cried as she listened.

Mrs. Diggins raised her enormous arms to lead us, and we gave the hymn a first try:

> "Let us break bread together on our knees (on our knees)
> Let us break bread together on our knees (on our knees)
> When I fall on my knees with my face to the rising sun
> O, Lord, have mercy on me (on me).
> O, Lord, have mercy on my soul (on my soul)
> O, Lord, have mercy on my soul (on my soul)
> When I fall on my knees with my face to the rising sun
> O, Lord, have mercy on my soul (on my soul)."

The first version was pretty miserable as we struggled to learn the tune, let alone the harmony. By the fifth rendition, I was so moved that I felt a lump forming in my throat, and I struggled to fight back tears. Even Mrs. Diggins's lids were half-closed as she continued to lead us.

I glanced over at John Malone. He wasn't singing. He never sang in music class, not for Mrs. Henderson and not now for Mrs. Diggins. Sometimes he moved his lips a little so that no one would catch on, but he definitely didn't sing. It wasn't like he was being bad or defiant like Robbie. It was more like he was just lost somewhere in his own world, too preoccupied to be roused by something as abstract, as exquisite, as a hymn.

Chapter 8

At least twice a week after school, I ventured to the bait shop. I had two missions in mind: to catch another glimpse of John Malone as he came to select his candy for the evening and to help Ezra close up his shop—by dusting, cleaning up the glass showcase, sorting out the coin rolls, or any other little chore that might assist him.

The first Monday after the long Thanksgiving weekend, John lingered in the bait shop longer than normal. Instead of zipping over to the candy counter, informing Ezra that he wanted to purchase "the usual," he drifted to the back of the shop where the fishing hats hung on a couple of nails hammered to the wall. This time, he wasn't kidding around as he tried on the hats. He looked as serious as a man intent on buying his first automobile.

Ezra winked at me from behind the front counter and moved to join him at the back of the store. "Hey, young John," he said with a smile, "are you in the market for a hat today?"

"Sort of," John nodded.

"That's good," Ezra said. "You looked mighty handsome in that first one you tried on. Just your size. Hang on while I find a mirror so that you can see how cool you look in it." He reached behind one of the shelves and pulled out a hand mirror while John retrieved the first hat and plopped it back on top of his head, pressing his bangs down even further into his eyes. "See there?" Ezra held the mirror up in front of him.

John smiled, pleased with the reflection.

I felt my own face grinning at the sight. Whenever John smiled, which wasn't often, his whole face changed, nearly all the tension draining out of it. In fact, watching John beaming at his own reflection in the mirror seemed so uncharacteristic that I really had to stop for a few seconds to consider if I really *had* ever seen him smile before.

But of course, I had. How could I forget his beautiful smile just a few days ago when I presented him with his free Slow Poke sucker? Or the many other times I'd seen him laughing with Bernard and some of the other boys?

The difference was that he was holding the smile longer than ever before. Usually, his grins faded so quickly that trying to observe one of them was like trying to watch a blink in motion. John seemed to catch himself whenever he smiled, and he'd stop suddenly, his mouth flattening out, his eyes shifting back to that suspicious, guarded look that was his trademark.

He was still beaming in the hand mirror, turning his head this way and that to admire the way the white canvas fishing hat, with the short brim all around it, framed his head. What a joy it was for me to see him like that! His transformed eyes were like those of a puppy, warm and innocent.

From my quiet place in the front of the store, I watched the two of them, John and Ezra, as they riffled through the other fishing hats. John laughed a few times as Ezra talked him through the selection. Finally, they decided on just the right one, which happened to be the first one John had tried on.

"Boy, you got a good eye!" Ezra said. "You honed in on the perfect choice right from the get-go!"

"You think it looks all right on me then?" John asked.

"I think it looks better than all right," Ezra said. He winked at me again. "I think you'll have the young ladies going wild when they get a load of you in that hat. But let's not take my word for it; let's test it out and see. Hey, Andi!" Ezra yelled across the room to me. "How you think John looks in this hat?"

I pretended that I was just casually looking up, seeing John in the hat for the first time. "It looks really cool on him, Ezra!" I smiled. "Fits him perfectly."

"See there?"

"How much is it?" John asked.

"Three dollars."

"Well, I can't buy it today," he said, his disappointment obvious as he dug into his side pocket to count his cash. "Can you hold it for me till next week, Ezra?"

"Sure thing, sure thing," he replied. "I'll put it right behind the front counter for you, whenever you're ready. You got a big fishing trip coming up?"

"Nah. My dad never has much time. I only went fishing once, but I liked it then pretty much."

"One time only! Tell you what. Come summertime, maybe you can come along with me and some of my buddies. Every summer, we take a week and go up to a really nice spot up on the river. More fish than you could imagine, so many that they almost jump right inside the boat without any wheedling from us."

"Cool!" John grinned again. "I'd like that. Just to get away from this place for a while."

Ezra nodded. But I noticed the way he was scrutinizing John, with troubled eyes. It was the same way Grandmom sometimes looked at me when she caught me gazing at Mama's photograph on the fireplace mantel.

About a half hour later, I was shining up the glass showcase with Windex, trying to remove all the greasy finger and handprints. Ezra was counting out his receipts.

Seth, sleepy-eyed, watched the last kid leave the shop and then began scratching the hardwood floor in preparation for his nap, scratching and scratching, until he finally whirled around three times the way dogs do before they finally plop down. Satisfied, he landed on the hard floor with a thud.

"Ezra, can I ask you something?"

"Shoot."

"Do you think God hears every single prayer?"

"You bet I do," he replied. "Somebody once said that 'prayer is God breathing in us.'"

I didn't say anything. Ezra had a habit of answering questions in a way that was far over my head, and sometimes I had to think about his responses for a long time, just so that I didn't say something stupid right after. I could feel him watching me from the corner of my eye.

"Why do you ask?

"If I tell you something, will you promise not to tell anyone?"

"Cross my heart," he said, his fingers tracing an X over his chest.

"I've been praying for a long time for God to tell me if there really is life after death. I just have to know!"

"Why you have to know so bad?"

"'Cause I miss my parents."

"I see," he said softly.

Seth was roused from his sleep by one of those inaudible noises that only dogs seem to hear. He sat up straight, ears cocked, and trotted into one of the aisles. Satisfied, he returned back to Ezra's side, scratched, and whirled three times again, before plopping back down on the floor.

"Anyway, I've been praying, on my mama's rosary beads, to be the next sixth grader to see—and actually *talk to*—Abraham Lincoln's ghost."

I thought Ezra might be shocked by my revelation. If he was, he didn't show it. Instead, he continued counting out his receipts through his half-glasses. "My, my," he said, "you sure picked a high and mighty ghost to try to hook up with."

"Well, Lincoln's ghost is supposed to be haunting our school, you know," I explained.

"No, I guess I didn't know that." He scratched his head, the long, loose braids moving in unison.

"But he only appears to sixth graders," I continued. "And I came really close to seeing him once too, right at the beginning of this school year. Howard Taylor and I were up in the auditorium after school, and we heard some really creepy sounds from a man coming from behind the stage. But when I pulled the curtain back, no one was there."

"And you think Lincoln's ghost was making those noises?"

"Who else could it have been? They were these low moans, a bunch of them in a row, and they didn't sound like noises any real man would be making for any reason I ever heard of." The words were gushing out of me now; I didn't even take a breath between them. "And nobody in the whole school could explain what the sounds were or who caused them!"

Ezra moved the corners of his mouth downward and nodded, as if my argument was a convincing one. "And you think if you meet up with Lincoln's ghost, he's gonna give you all the answers you're looking for, huh?"

"I figure if I can talk to a real ghost, then there must definitely be life after death," I said.

"You got a point there."

"Besides, I don't know any other ghost to ask. Do you?"

"No, I sure don't know no ghosts." He chuckled softly.

I moved around from the glass showcase, my work finished there, and began sorting out some more of the coin rolls. The two of us worked at our respective jobs for a while, side by side, without either of us uttering a word. I knew Ezra well enough by now to be able to tell when he could listen to me and when he really needed to concentrate on what he was doing. He was working his adding machine, running up a long tape, and when he finally finished, he pulled off his half-glasses and began rubbing his eyes.

"Ezra?" I said softly. "Do *you* believe there's life after death?"

He looked me straight in the eye, not a glimmer of a smile on his lips. "I'm no ghost," he said, "but for what it's worth, I'm here to tell you that life goes on after death. I'm absolutely convinced of it."

"But how do you know!?" I felt my heart accelerating. My fingers were too tingly to keep rolling up the coins, so I stopped. "You've got to tell me everything you know about it!"

"Not so fast, little girl," he said, laughing and holding up both palms flat in front of me. "There's a whole bunch of reasons why I believe life goes on."

"A whole bunch!"

"Tell you what—I'll give you one reason a month, from now till the end of the school year. How's that?"

"One reason a month!" I moaned. "Why can't you just tell me all of them right now?"

"'Cause I want you to think about them really good, each one of them. Besides, if I tell them to you all at once, you ain't gonna remember none of them. Trust me, one at a time is better. And maybe, by the end of the school year, you'll even come up with some reasons of your own."

"Can I at least hear the first one today?"

"I think that would only be fair," he said with a smile.

I could hardly wait. I scrunched down on the floor beside Seth and began stroking his fur while I waited for the first mystery to be revealed, my eyes wide with anticipation. Knowing Ezra and the difficult way he phrased things, I knew this wasn't going to be easy. Still, I wanted to catch and savor each and every word.

"One reason I believe that life goes on," he began, "is because the desire for an afterlife is right there, smack dab in the middle of all of our hearts. Each of us instinctively hungers for something better—purer, kinder—than this world offers us. Why do you think that would be? All of us yearning for the exact same thing? Ecclesiastes comes right out and says that God put 'eternity in our hearts.' Why would God go ahead and do that if there's no such thing?"

I exhaled a deep breath, kind of like a balloon deflating. It wasn't exactly the bombshell I'd been hungering for, but I knew it would have to do for now.

"Just think about it," he said.

"I will. I promise," I said slowly. "But if that's really true, then how come—"

My question was interrupted by an abrupt sound. Ezra and I turned to our left, toward the front door, only to find John Malone standing there. Seth's tail began thumping against the counter, and he rushed over to welcome him by licking his hand.

Seth didn't seem startled by John's surprise appearance, but I was. Mostly, I wondered why we hadn't heard the bells when he first opened the front door.

Looking at Ezra, he held up three dollar bills. "Is it too late to buy that hat today?"

Chapter 9

When John Malone donned that white fishing hat, he became a whole new man. I guessed it was just one of those unexplainable phenomena, like the way people gravitate to the sides of an elevator rather than standing in the center. He walked with conviction and talked with animation; even his slouchy posture grew more erect.

I noticed all of that straight off the bat, just by observing him in the schoolyard the next morning before the bell rang. John was jostling with Bernard and some of the other boys as they stood in a huddle, laughing together at times. His eyes were intense, more engaged than before. And all this just because of a fishing hat. It was hard to believe.

When he showed up wearing the hat to class, I thought for sure that Mr. Banner would swipe it right off of his head. But for some reason, he didn't. Maybe Mr. Banner, too, could see its positive influence on John. At any rate, as luck would have it, he acquired the hat just in time for his oral report.

Setting the tone for John's essay at half past two in the afternoon, Mr. Banner posed a question to the class: "Whose death affects us more than any other in our history?" A bunch of hands rose in the air. Mr. Banner chose to call on Howard.

"Our own?" Howard replied.

Mr. Banner looked taken aback for one quick second, and a slow smile formed on his face. "Well, I guess you would be right about that one," he said. He began to chuckle softly and then laughed out loud. "You *are* quite the philosopher, aren't you? What I was going for, of course, was Abraham Lincoln's death. But Howard's answer is absolutely the correct one." Although he appeared to be fighting to suppress it, he began snickering again.

It was refreshing to see Mr. Banner laugh, though we were all kind of stumped as to what was so funny. Still, the sight and sound of his laughter was a treat we had never witnessed before.

Controlling himself, he drew out a long sigh, as if that too felt good to him. "Okay then," he said. "Mr. Malone, I believe it's time for our next Lincoln report, and I believe that you're the one who'll be presenting it to us. Your assigned topic was Lincoln's dreams. Is that correct?"

John nodded, shifting his shoulders around to limber himself up before he rose from his chair. Then he walked up to the head of the class, his head tilted downward. In his hand, he held a small index card.

I felt nervous for him, but John didn't seem to be the least bit scared. He fingered the brim of his hat before he began. "My report," he said, "is about two dreams that Abraham Lincoln had shortly before he was assassinated. The first dream foreshadowed his own death."

I noticed several of the kids scooting forward in their seats, some with their chins resting in the palms of their hands, eager to hear the story.

"Everything that I'm going to read to you," John continued, "is an actual quote from Ward Hill Lamon. Lamon was an old friend of Lincoln's, and when Lincoln became president, he appointed Ward Hill Lamon to a security position in the White House.

"Lamon really guarded Lincoln's safety with a lot of energy and devotion. In fact, he even quit a couple of times in frustration because Lincoln didn't take enough precautions about his own safety. So it really bugged him that he wasn't there to protect Lincoln on the night he died, especially since Lincoln had told him about this dream a few days before. But on the night Lincoln died, he had sent Lamon away on another assignment in Virginia."

What a luxury it was to be able to gaze at John Malone's face, in all its glorious detail, to my heart's content! I found it difficult to concentrate on what he was saying, I was so engrossed in studying the shape of his eyes, the different shades of color in his brown hair, and the way his eyebrows, peaking through his bangs, raised and lowered when he pronounced certain words.

"Lamon never got over his guilt," John said. "Anyway, what I'm about to read to you is exactly what Abraham Lincoln supposedly told Lamon a few days before he was killed."

John looked down at the index card and began reciting Lincoln's words:

"About ten days ago, I retired late. I soon began to dream. There seemed to be a deathlike stillness about me. Then I heard subdued sobs, as if a number of people were weeping. I thought I left my bed and wandered downstairs. There the silence was broken by the same pitiful sobbing, but the mourners were invisible. I went from room to room; no living person was in sight, but the same mournful sounds of distress met me as I passed along. It was light in all the rooms; every object was familiar to me, but where were all the people who were grieving as if their hearts would break? I was puzzled and alarmed. What could be the meaning of all this? Determined to find the cause of a state of things so mysterious and shocking, I kept on until I arrived at the East Room, which I entered. Before me was a cat-a-f, cat-a-fal . . ."

"Catafalque," Mr. Banner said, coming to his aide. "It means a temporary wooden framework, usually built for a coffin to be placed upon. Go on, John."

"Before me was a catafalque," John repeated, "on which rested a corpse wrapped in funeral vestments. Around it were stationed soldiers who were acting as guards; and there was a throng of people, some gazing mournfully at the corpse, whose face was covered, others weeping pitifully. 'Who is dead in the White House?' I demanded of one of the soldiers. 'The President,' was his answer. 'He was killed by an assassin.' Then came a loud burst of grief from the crowd, which woke me from my dream. I slept no more that night, and although it was only a dream, I have been strangely annoyed by it ever since."

John looked up from the index card. "A few days later, President Lincoln was murdered by John Wilkes Booth." He looked at Mr. Banner.

"I wish you wouldn't have just read Lincoln's words to us verbatim," Mr. Banner said. "But it was still a fine accounting of his dream nevertheless. Continue."

"Lincoln also had a second dream just before his death," John said. "On the night before he was shot, he had the same dream that he'd had two times before."

"That's correct," Mr. Banner said.

"Lincoln considered it a good dream, but it beats me why he did." John shook his head. "In this dream, he was all alone on a ship in the middle of the ocean. He had no oars, no rudder, and he was drifting further and further out to sea. He had no idea where he was heading. But Lincoln said he had that dream whenever something wonderful was about to happen."

Though the second dream wasn't as creepy as the first one, I agreed with John. If I had a dream that I was drifting out to sea all by myself with no way to stop or turn around, I'd be terrified. Then again, I don't know how to swim.

"Very good," Mr. Banner said as he checked off the list of oral report objectives he used to determine our grade. Judging by the flair with which he did it, we could tell that John had received an excellent grade.

Mrs. Diggins spent the next several music classes preparing us for the Christmas pageant. As tradition dictated, each year the entire school performed in ascending order, with the sixth graders always presenting the grand finale.

At first, I dreaded the thought of remaining after school till 5:00 p.m. twice a week for the next two weeks just so that we could practice the four carols our class was assigned to perform. It meant less time with Ezra.

"Oh, what a tangled web we weave when first we practice to deceive" was a platitude that Grandmom recited often. One day the week before, Grandmom had already woken up from her nap by the time I got home, and I told her I was late because I had been at choir practice. Now I really *did* have choir practice and couldn't visit Ezra. What a conundrum!

For the first time in my life, I was lying to Grandmom. I felt lower than a worm, but I had to do it. If she ever found out I was visiting the bait shop after school, it was a virtual certainty that she would forbid me right then and there, no questions asked, no explanations necessary, and I would never see Ezra again. And so, not telling Grandmom about it in the first place was my only option.

By the following week, we had graduated from performing our carols in the music room to actually practicing on the stage of the auditorium. "It's all about acoustics," Mrs. Diggins informed us. "You'll be amazed how much better you all sound when you're up on that stage."

She was right. Although our rendition of "God Rest Ye Merry Gentlemen" usually sounded flat and boring, the harmonies came alive when we stood on the stage in the auditorium. From my place in the second row—the sopranos in front of me and the altos behind—I could barely hear my own voice as it melded into the others, a link in a wondrous chain of multidimensional sound.

It was difficult to look at John Malone while we were performing, but every once in a while, I'd tilt my head way toward the left, where John was standing in the back row, and I could spot him, moving his lips, but still not singing, his eyes darting around the stage, up toward the flood lights and then to the exit doors on each side. Mrs. Diggins was not as generous as Mr. Banner when it came to his fishing hat. The first day he wore it to music class, she laid down the law: either he would take it off, or else she'd take it off for him.

It was nearly four-thirty in the afternoon when we wrapped up our practice performance that Monday. I was packing my book bag near the back of the stage when someone tapped me on my shoulder from behind. When I turned around, I was shocked to discover that it was John Malone!

Most all of the other kids were already gone, or too busy to notice. "Is it true that you and Howard nearly cornered Lincoln's ghost up here?" he asked.

Like in the bait shop, I remained startled and tongue-tied. All I could muster was a nod.

Mrs. Diggins had stepped down from the stage and was stuffing the sheet music into her large briefcase resting on the gymnasium floor. "If you children would hand these pages back to me neatly, like human beings, instead of every which way like pigs . . ." she bemoaned, more or less to herself.

John lowered his voice to a whisper. "I've been checking the stage out for the last week before and after gym class," he said. "And tonight, before we started to practice, I went behind the stage again. There's a little spiral staircase back there, and when you walk up, there's just a small area with one chair in front of a round window. When you leave school tonight, look up at the very top of the building. At the highest point near the roof, you'll notice that there's a little round window. Anyway, I bet that's where Lincoln's ghost hides out."

"Why do you say that?" I had finally managed to come up with a complete sentence in John's presence. *This* was progress!

He moved in even closer, trying to avoid the scrutiny of Mrs. Diggins. I could smell the spearmint gum on his breath. "Because you can tell that somebody's hiding out in that little space."

"How do you know?" I asked excitedly.

"Because I tricked him," he said.

"You tricked Abraham Lincoln?"

"Yup, after gym class last Friday, I snuck in there and moved some things around. Nothing anyone would notice. I just pushed the chair over to the left a little bit, and stuff like that."

"And?"

"And tonight, not only was the chair moved way further to the right, but there was an old blanket lying beside it. Someone definitely goes into that little space on a regular basis."

The emotions were banging around inside of me like bumper cars at the carnival. Here was John Malone, actually standing right in front of me, and we were having our first in-depth conversation! He had just made me privy to the actual hiding place of Abraham Lincoln's ghost! And that hiding place was only a few feet away from where we were standing right at that very moment! Ecstasy and fear both were raging inside of me.

"I know you want to try to stalk Lincoln's ghost," John continued. "So, if you want, I can help you, 'cause you're probably afraid to do it all by yourself . . ."

Now that I was getting used to the fact that John Malone was talking to me, my brain was beginning to function again. How did he know so much about it? I wondered. How did he know that I wanted to talk to Lincoln's ghost? Nobody alive knew that secret.

Except Ezra.

Before I could respond, our serious discussion had captured the attention of Mrs. Diggins. She snapped her briefcase shut. "Now, what are you two plotting about?" she asked, moving toward us suspiciously, her high heels clacking on the lacquered gym floor. The sound echoed in the large room, reverberating as if there were ten Mrs. Digginses approaching us. It was all about acoustics, I thought absent-mindedly.

John slapped his fishing hat back on his head and then tilted it forward, over his eyes, Frank Sinatra-style. "We're just talking," he said.

Even better than the prospect of hunting Lincoln's ghost with him, another thought was crossing my mind. I was savoring the distinct possibility that John Malone might actually be starting to like me back. Why else would he be going through all this trouble?

"Well, talk outside, or talk on your way home, but don't talk on my time," Mrs. Diggins said. "It's late now, and pretty soon, it's gonna be dark outside." She was waving her long fingernails around in the air, the third button on her blouse popping open in the process. "And if you come home after dark, both of your parents are gonna be all over me like ants on a picnic."

"Think about it," John said to me, slipping on his winter coat. With that, he rushed out of the auditorium.

Think about it? What a silly thing to say. It would be difficult to think about anything else.

"Well, don't just stand there grinning!" Mrs. Diggins yelped. "Put on your coat, and get your little butt home!"

Chapter 10

John Malone's sudden interest had the same glorious effect on me as his fishing hat had on him. Like Lincoln's piano, I was nearly levitating during the walk to school the next morning. I felt warm down to my toes, even though the temperature was well below freezing and the forecast called for a winter storm advisory.

As soon as I reached the school and spotted Alfreda, I grabbed her arm, bursting with my unbelievable news. But before I could get it out, even one word, we noticed a group of kids beginning to gather on the far end of the schoolyard. Within seconds, the size of the huddle had multiplied before our eyes.

"What on earth do you think is going on?" Alfreda said.

Curious, we headed toward the group. From between the shoulders of an excited crowd, now nearly a dozen deep all around, I spotted the heads of Keely and Bertha Riggs bobbing in the center. Moving in to get a closer look, I was stunned by what I saw. Both of their winter coats were peeled off, and Bertha was beating Keely in the chest and face like a heavyweight boxer. Keely's hands were up in front of her nose, her wrists shaking as she desperately tried to land a return punch.

"It's Keely!" I gasped. "We've got to help her!"

"No, Andi!" Alfreda said, pulling me back. "If you mess with Bertha Riggs, you're gonna be her next target!"

Some kids were yelling at Bertha to stop, but most of them were egging her on, or choosing sides. From the sidelines came the assorted shouts.

"Punch her back, Keely!"

"Hit her harder, Bertha! *Harder!*"

"Keely is a great big chicken. Bawk, bawk, bawk!"

Finally, big, slow tears began to stream down Keely's cheeks. Seeing her cry was the impetus Bertha needed to pull out all the stops. Her mouth of jagged teeth flew open, and her eyes bulged wide enough that I could see the whites all around her pupils. She looked like a rabid animal, both of her fists flying, her face engorged with hatred.

Keely was screaming, wailing.

I couldn't stand it. Bolting from the crowd, I ran inside the school to summon a teacher. Unfortunately, the first one I found was dainty Miss Burden, the first-grade teacher, sipping a cup of orange juice as she strolled toward her classroom.

"You have to come quick!" I grabbed her arm, spilling the juice in the process. "There's a big fight outside! You've got to come and stop it—*now!*"

She pulled herself free from me, not from indifference to my plea, but from fear, or maybe just distraction caused by the new orange stain marring her pink lace sleeve. "Mr. Alphonse is in there," she said, pointing to the secretary's office, her eyes widening. "Go get him!"

Overhearing, Mr. Alphonse dropped the stack of papers he was carrying. They fluttered across the hardwood floor like a deck of cards. Before I could even move a step, he was already running toward the entrance, out toward the schoolyard.

When we reached the crowd, I pushed my way to the front. Keely was on the ground sobbing hysterically, her nose bloody, while Bertha sat on top of her, pummeling her. Keely was not even trying to fight back anymore; she lay against the cold ground, limp and cornered.

Her immobility didn't lessen Bertha's rage one bit. Instead, Bertha was crazed. She hammered at Keely's chest until she ripped her white cotton blouse completely off her body. "Look!" someone shouted. "Keely's training bra is showing! Keely's nearly naked!"

Mr. Alphonse was shoving through the mass of kids as fast as he could.

Buoyed by the heckling, or maybe because she saw Mr. Alphonse approaching from the corner of her eye, Bertha waged one final humiliation against Keely. With fingers curled like claws and a maniacal glint in her black eyes, she tore off Keely's bra.

There was a stunned gasp from the crowd. Then some shouts, hoots, jeers. Finally, there was just laughter—the kind of ugly hysteria that only a mob can make.

I knew I'd never forget the look on Keely's face at that moment for as long as I lived. Throughout the fight, her gaze—fixed on Bertha—had been one of sheer terror. But the moment she was stripped in front of the taunting crowd, it was as if an electric current short-circuited her soul, and her eyes went completely dead. A sharp pain ripped my heart, shredding it like ribbons.

Mr. Alphonse was finally able to get a good enough grip on Bertha to yank her up by the shoulders and shove her off of Keely. "Stop it! You're going to kill her!" he shouted. Since her fists could no longer reach Keely, Bertha began spitting at her. "Stop it!" he screamed again. "Are you *crazy*?"

Mr. Jackson had joined him by now. It took the two of them to restrain Bertha, who was jumping and thrashing like a wild bronco. Mr. Banner was the next to arrive on the scene. He knelt over Keely gently, like she was a wounded kitten, shielding her with his body and covering her bare chest with his own suit coat. "Get out of here, all of you!" he screamed at the crowd. "You should all be ashamed of yourselves! Get to class and stop gawking!"

But school was the last place I wanted to be. The only thing I could think to do was to run away, as fast as my wobbly legs would carry me, straight to the bait shop.

The snow was already beginning to fall in thick, wet flakes by the time I reached the front steps. With frozen fingers, I pulled the door open, the brass bells clanging. As usual, the sound was enough to capture Ezra's attention. He was assisting an old black gentleman in choosing a new fishing pole, but when he saw me, he excused himself and walked toward me.

"What are you thinking, little girl?" he said, looking up at the black-enamel clock hanging over the cash register. "You should be in school."

I burst into tears, clinging to him.

"Now what have we here?" he asked. I could feel Seth sidle up behind me, his tail wagging as he sniffed my backside.

"That's okay, E-Z," the old black man said to Ezra. "You take care of that little white girl, while I just keep on looking here. I'm in no hurry, so don't bother yourself none with me just yet."

Now that I had given into the urge to weep, it felt like I might never stop. It had been a long, long time since I had allowed myself to sob, and now I knew why. Sometimes succumbing to a cry was like breaking down a levy; the next thing you know, you're engulfed in a torrent of sorrow that feels like it might wash you away. I could hear my own convulsive gasps as I wept in Ezra's arms. It was a frightening sound, even to me.

"Andi Powell," he grabbed me by each of my shoulders, calling out my name as if he was trying to rouse me from the depths of my agony. He looked me square in the eye. "Andi Powell," he said again, "what on earth has got you so upset?"

I tried to speak but couldn't.

"Take a deep breath," Ezra instructed. I did just what he said. "Good," he said, smiling, his beautiful white teeth appearing. "Now another one."

I sucked in several deep breaths of air, until, eventually, the sobs turned into chokes that sounded more like hiccups. Seth was right beside me, his head cocked slightly and his brown eyes gazing at me as if he too was worried.

"Better now?" Ezra asked.

I nodded, took one more deep breath without being coaxed, and sat down on the floor. Slowly, I began my tale, telling Ezra all about the fight between Keely and Bertha, every single, grizzly detail that I could recall. In the retelling, especially when I got to the part when Bertha ripped off her clothes, I started to cry all over again. Seth began licking my face, his saliva warm and sticky.

"Uh-uh-uhmmm," the old black man said from among the fishing poles, clicking his teeth. "Sounds like that little girl damn near killed the other one."

"Do you think she's gonna die?" I asked, looking up at Ezra.

"Naw," he replied. "She won't die. She'll just be bruised up for a while."

"Don't that just beat everything," the old man said as he shook his head and lit up a cigarette. "Two little girls going at each other like that. Now what on earth could cause one little girl to be so dang mad at another little girl? Don't make no sense to me. This world's going nuts, if you ask me. Uh-uh-uhmmm."

A few more shallow gasps came out of me; I was all cried out. Suddenly, I felt exhausted, drained, as if I had just finished running a 100-mile marathon and had not one ounce of strength left in my body. But I also felt a strange peace washing over me all of a sudden, comforted beyond my expectations, almost dizzy with comfort. The beautiful snow falling outside and the warmth of being inside Ezra's shop at the beginning of a school day—not to mention being with Ezra himself—gave me the same feeling as when Grandmom wrapped a towel around me, clean and fresh from the dryer, on cold winter nights.

Ezra was back by the old man's side, showing him something about one of the thingamabobs hanging on the pegboard, whatever it was. They were an odd pair—Ezra, lean and striking, and the old man, bent and weathered, his face pockmarked, the whites of his eyes yellowed. He was dressed in suspenders and a worn flannel shirt. Ezra, adorned in a khaki tunic, was such a handsome man, of course, in his dazzling, unconventional way. As I watched him and the old man converse, I was newly struck by Ezra's gracefulness when he moved, graceful in a masculine way, like a racehorse. His body just flowed, his hands moving together in fluid rhythm whenever he gestured.

It took me a while to remember that I was angry at him for violating my confidence with John Malone. Even though John's learning my secret had opened the door to his new interest in me, it still didn't justify Ezra breaking his promise to keep it confidential.

"I've got a real bone to pick with you, Ezra!" I said, folding my arms and glaring at him.

"Now, why're you mad at me all of a sudden?" he asked, looking at the old man and throwing up his palms. "Ain't that just like a woman? Don't matter how big or small they are, they're all the same. There's just no predicting them! One minute they're coming to you for some solace; the very next minute, they're turning on you."

The old man chuckled, a low, scratchy sound that went deep enough in his throat to trigger a cough. "Ain't that the truth," he rasped.

I wasn't certain whether I was supposed to laugh along with them or whether making a joke of it had further enraged me. Stroking Seth's hair in confusion, I remained silent.

"So, why're you mad?" Ezra asked again, walking toward me.

I eyed the old man with annoyance. This was a private matter between me and Ezra, and his presence was beginning to be a nuisance. Why was he buying a fishing pole in the dead of winter anyway? I hesitated to continue as long as he was still there in the shop, eavesdropping on our every word. But from the looks of his slow gait and meticulous scrutiny of every fishing rod in the place, it didn't appear that he was going anywhere anytime soon. I decided I could outsmart him.

"I'm mad at you," I began, "because you told—J. M.—my secret when I asked you not to."

"J. M.? Secret?" Ezra scratched one of his thick braids. "What the heck you talkin' about, little girl?"

I leaned closer to him. "J. M. is John Malone," I whispered.

"Ohhh," Ezra nodded in recognition. Then his face clouded again. "What secret did I tell Joh—" He stopped himself. "What secret did I tell—J. M.?"

"About me and . . . you know." I leaned closer to him again, whispering, "About my wanting to talk to—L. G."

"L. G.?"

The old man started chortling again from the other side of the aisle, but Ezra kept a straight face.

"*You* know," I prompted, "Lincoln's G.? Remember? Remember what Howard and I thought we heard in the auditorium?"

Ezra thought for a long while before it finally dawned on him what I was trying to say. "Ohh!" he smiled, "I get it now! . . . But I most certainly did not violate your confidence, little girl. I didn't say one word about you and—L. G.—to J. M. or anyone else. I swear on a stack of Bibles."

"You didn't?" I believed Ezra all right. Especially since he had brought the Bible into it. Ezra used the Bible like travelers used maps. I knew he would never take *that* book in vain. Not ever. "Then, how do you suppose he knew?" I asked.

Ezra shrugged and furrowed his brow. Although he tried to make it a gesture of great gravity and consequence, I could tell he had little pathos for my mystery. He winked at the old man as he crossed back over to where he was standing, pulling out a fishing pole that was on the top shelf, too high for the bent old man to reach. Ezra began explaining something about how it was different from the one the old man was holding, the one he wanted to purchase.

Now that Ezra and I were square again, I no longer minded the old man's presence. I kind of liked the sound of his bass voice; it reminded me of the guy with the deepest voice in the Four Tops or The Temptations. "Hey, mister," I called out to him from across the room. "Why're you buying a fishing pole in the wintertime?"

"Huh?" The old man looked up at me from the middle of the merchandise he was selecting. "Because, little miss, I'm going to be doing me some ice fishing, you understand?"

"You need to get you a rod that has large guides, a sensitive tip, something that has some real backbone," Ezra continued, coaching the old man in his selection. "You're also gonna need a four- to eight-pound test ice-line. And an assortment of split-shot and bobber stops with beads."

To me, it was as if he was talking a foreign language, but the old man was nodding his head in agreement. "So you think I'd be better off buying that one, huh, E-Z?" he asked Ezra. Then he looked over at me, chuckling and coughing again. "Damn, all these initials here are getting me hungry for some alphabet soup! I'm gonna have to get me home P-D-Q!"

But the old man did anything but leave the shop quickly. Instead, he hemmed and hawed about the supplies for his ice fishing expedition for over an hour. Five other customers came and went, and he was still standing in the aisle, smoking his cigarettes like they were made out of candy, fingering each and every fishing rod until he could come to a decision.

Finally, his new pole wrapped snugly in heavy brown paper, he left the bait shop. It was nearly lunchtime. I knew I'd have to leave soon. Any minute, the kids would be arriving to buy their lunchtime candy, and I didn't want to be seen. I could still get home in time to watch soap operas with Grandmom for the rest of the afternoon.

Ezra sat down on the high stool behind the register. I was crouched on the floor a few feet away, still caressing Seth. By that time, I was feeling miserable again. I couldn't get the image of Keely's eyes, after her bra had been stripped off, out of my head. Never had I seen such a lifeless look in anyone's eyes. It was an image I knew I'd never get out of my head, even if I lived to be a hundred.

I wondered where Keely was now, what she was doing, if she was all right. I wondered what happened after Mr. Banner scooped her off the ground as tenderly as a stillborn baby. What could she be thinking now? How could she face ever coming back to class again after enduring such public humiliation? Then I'd see her face in my mind again, her brown eyes filling up with so much suffering that they finally just broke.

Ezra seemed to know what I was thinking, just like he knew everything else. He was quiet for a long time, his expression serious and sad. "Pretty rough stuff, huh?" he said to me softly.

I nodded.

"Hate is an awfully powerful thing," he said. "But just try to remember, love is even stronger."

"How can that be?" I asked. "Keely is good and loving, and Bertha is mean and hateful. But it was Bertha who *won* the fight."

"That she did," he said with a nod, looking even sadder. Seth got up from beside me and moved toward his master, plunking down beside him on the floor. "Listen," Ezra said, "I know a thing or two about the Riggs family . . . Bertha's daddy is in prison for armed robbery, and her mama is a drug addict who up and ran off a few years back. Since then, Bertha takes turns living with her aunties. One of her aunties' boyfriends used to smack her around. Slammed her into the wall once, almost broke her jaw. He did manage to chip most of her front teeth. How you think she got to looking like that?"

I crossed my arms against my chest tightly as if the gesture could make me stop listening to what he was saying. I didn't know what to think. He was trying to get me to see things from Bertha's point of view—I understood that—but I was way too angry to even consider feeling sorry for her.

Ezra always made things so complicated. With him, there were no good guys and bad guys. No black and white. His was a world of endless shades in between, kind of like our hands on the playground that day.

"What about Keely?" I protested.

"Keely got a bad deal all right," he replied. "Bad things happen to good people sometimes; there's just no doubt about it. People do all kinds of terrible things to one another. That's been going on since the beginning of time, and that ain't ever gonna stop, I'm afraid."

I was silent. I saw Keely's eyes dying again in my head.

"I think something bad happened to your friend John Malone too," Ezra said.

Now he had my full attention. "Like what?"

Ezra shrugged. "Hard telling what. Just a feeling I have, that's all."

"Sometimes I have that feeling about him too," I admitted. "He never sings in music class, you know."

"But that doesn't mean we give up on people," Ezra continued, "just because they do something mean or have something mean done to them. That's where love comes in. And somehow, it all works itself out in the end."

"Like how?" I wondered.

Ignoring my question, Ezra rose from his chair. Opening the top drawer of a cabinet beside the cash register, he retrieved a rawhide bone for Seth and placed it into his eager jaws. The shepherd fluttered his tail in gratitude. Yawning, Ezra stretched his arms high into the air. "It's really coming down out there," he said, peering out the window at the accumulating snow. At least four inches blanketed the ground. "Look at that sad, old, dead tree blowing around in the cold, would you?" He pointed to a gargantuan oak on the other side of the street. "Just look at all those dead limbs sticking up there in the air. Makes me hurt just to look at it . . . You figure you can help me chop it down first chance we get?"

"Chop it down?" I crinkled my nose. "That tree's not dead, Ezra. It's just wintertime! Come spring, it'll be just fine again."

"You think so, huh?" he said, reaching under the counter and handing me a Slow Poke sucker.

I nodded.

"You figure maybe Bertha and Keely are just going through their own wintertime too?" he asked.

Now I knew what he was doing. He was saying one of those riddle-like things again, to try to make me think, one of those things that I thought about so long and hard after I left the bait shop that sometimes my head started to ache.

"Everything that goes to sleep wakes up again," he said. "Now, why would that be?"

I was silent.

"It's called resurrection," he said. "Nighttime gives way to the dawn of morning. Wintertime gives way to spring. It's all a pattern, don't you think?"

I nodded.

"By the way," he smiled, "that's another reason why I believe there's life after death."

Chapter 11

The next day was Wednesday, three days before Christmas vacation. Before I even hung my parka on the hook in the girl's closet, I handed Mr. Banner the excuse that Grandmom had written, informing him that I had become ill after I witnessed the fight and asking him to please excuse me for my absence. Scanning the note quickly, Mr. Banner's eyes swelled with a distracted sadness. He crumpled the note and nodded at me as if he understood.

Though I was half-expecting it, the sight of Keely's vacant desk still stunned me. I took my seat and stared at its eerie emptiness—her pencil box and little packet of tissues stood near the opening of her desk, and further back, her textbooks waited. Like a silent shrine, it stirred an emotion that was similar to what I felt the first time I saw my parents' tombstone with their names and dates engraved in the granite—a tangible reminder of an essential presence lost.

Bertha arrived just before the bell rang, nothing but a small scratch on her left cheek. She took her seat quickly and quietly. At first, I thought she had learned something, maybe, from her evil act and was contrite, but after just a few minutes, she was her old self again, flicking saliva paper balls at her friend Linda Walker from across the room.

I stared at Bertha now, at her jagged teeth and nappy, dirty hair. I was trying hard not to hate her, but part of me still did. I kept thinking about what Ezra had told me about her family yesterday. She was mean all right, but pitiable too. I knew how lonely it could be to live without your parents. I tried to imagine Bertha being thrown against a wall hard enough to break her teeth, with nobody there to comfort her. How devastated she must have been when she saw her reflection in the mirror afterward. How sad it was that no one cared enough to fix her teeth, and she had to live her life looking like that. No wonder she didn't smile much.

I asked everyone what he or she knew about Keely and when she was returning to school, but no one knew anything. All they could tell me was that she never came to class yesterday and that Bertha had gotten a stern enough paddling from Principal Mortenson to make her cry. Bertha had later reappeared in class still whimpering, they said, but by recess, she was back to bragging on the playground about her victory, her ebony eyes shining as she recounted the gory details one by one, basking in Keely's degradation over being beaten and stripped in front of a gawking crowd.

The only joy for me in returning to class was the sublime sight of John Malone in his fishing hat, wearing a new navy blue velveteen shirt. From beneath the white rim of his cap, his bangs hung even longer over his eyebrows, well into his eyes. They were about as long as his father allowed his bangs to get before he grabbed his shears and trimmed them back himself. I overhead him telling Bernard about it the first time it happened: "Whenever my dad screams, 'Get me the goddamned shears!'" he had said, "I know I'm in big trouble." On those days, John would arrive at school with his black eyebrows clear in view, looking younger, rawer, defeated. On those days, he never made eye contact with anyone.

But today, with his bangs flowing, he was confident and focused. I kept waiting for him to turn around and look at me, like boys do when they like you, but he never looked back in my direction, not even a glance. Maybe he had forgotten all about me in the last twenty-four hours. Maybe everything that we had built up to on Monday was over. Out of sight, out of mind does happen, I guess, though I couldn't imagine ever forgetting about him.

That's when I suddenly noticed another disturbing development. After my single day of absence, Roxanna Trixler was batting her baby blues at John again. All morning long, she was at it, fluttering her lashes his way and then twirling her long hair with her index finger. Fluttering and twirling. Twirling and fluttering. My heart pinched when he finally looked over at her just before recess and smiled. She beamed at him and then fluttered some more.

I decided, from that point on, that I hated John Malone.

"It's time for our last oral report on Lincoln's ghost," Mr. Banner announced later that afternoon. "Since we didn't keep our usual schedule yesterday because of . . ." He looked over at Bertha, his voice breaking off. "Well, suffice it to say that we're doing oral reports today instead of yesterday. Howard, you're on."

Howard Taylor was wearing his best bow tie for the occasion, a maroon one, with socks to match, of course. "My report, unlike all the others that were simply a prelude, is *really* about Lincoln's ghost," he began.

It might have seemed an arrogant statement had anyone other than Howard said it. But we all understood that it was merely his superior brain talking, that he was much too sweet to willingly utter an offensive word to anyone.

"The truth is, since his death in 1865," he continued, "there have been numerous sightings of Abraham Lincoln's ghost. In fact, Lincoln's ghost is probably among the most prevalent ghosts in all of our nation's history. Some of the places that his ghost has been spotted, besides our very own school, are . . . at Fort Monroe in Virginia, at Ford's Theater where he was killed, at the White House during several administrations, and last but not least, his tomb in Springfield, where—I remind you—we will be visiting at the end of this school year. There is even a legend that says, every April on the anniversary of his assassination, a phantom train can be seen traveling along the same route as his original funeral train, from Washington through New York State to his final resting place in Springfield, Illinois."

I had to wonder, was it the story he was telling or Howard's delivery that was so compelling? Probably both. Not that I expected any less from him. Howard Taylor was, indisputably, the most intelligent student in both sixth-grade classes combined.

"In fact," Howard continued, gesturing with one index finger high in the air like a politician on television might do, "often in the month of April, the funeral train appears on the tracks around Urbana, Illinois, draped in black crepe. Through the windows, some have claimed to see grinning skeletons in blue coats, just like the Northern soldiers used to wear in the Civil War. And, near the middle of the train, some have reportedly seen the coffins of both Lincoln and his son Willie. After the phantom train passes, clocks in the area are often five to ten minutes behind. Others have reported seeing Lincoln and Willie walking off the train, hand in hand."

We were all spellbound. And Howard could tell. "Allow me to inform you now," he said, the bravado in his voice escalating the drama of his words, "about some of the numerous other sightings of his ghost. The first person to actually report seeing the ghost of Abraham Lincoln was the wife of President Calvin Coolidge, who was president from 1923 through 1929. First Lady Grace Coolidge claims to have walked in on Lincoln's ghost, deep in thought, staring out a window of the Oval Office toward the Potomac River, his hands clasped behind his back. She was fond of telling overnight visitors that when the light over the front door at the White House was dimmed for the evening, the ghost of Abraham Lincoln paced back and forth on the north porch of the White House."

"And that's not all," Howard said, peering at us over his glasses, his eyebrows arching high in the air. "Queen Wilhelmina of the Netherlands also saw Lincoln's ghost while she was a guest at the White House during Franklin Roosevelt's term in office. During the night, she heard a knock at her bedroom door. When she opened it, there he was—Abraham Lincoln, just standing there looking at her. She fainted, of course. Religious leader Norman Vincent Peale also claims that a famous actor, who he will not name, saw Lincoln's ghost when he was a guest at the White House. This actor woke up to hear someone calling for help. He sat up in his bed only to see—and I quote Norman Vincent Peale—'the lanky form of Lincoln prostrate on the floor in prayer, arms outstretched with fingers digging into the carpet.'"

A hand shot up. It belonged to, of all people, Robbie Taggert. "What does that word mean—prostrate?"

Howard looked at Mr. Banner.

"You know, don't you, Howard?" he said.

Howard nodded.

"Then by all means, go for it!"

"It means lying flat out on the floor, usually from surrender or exhaustion."

"As usual, a very correct and thorough answer," Mr. Banner said. "Carry on."

"During another time in the Lincoln bedroom," he said, "A female employee of Eleanor Roosevelt—some say it was her maid; some say her secretary—at any rate, this woman saw Lincoln sitting on the bed in the Lincoln bedroom pulling off his boots."

"Pee-yew!" Robbie Taggert interjected. "After wearing them for over a hundred years, I'll bet they really stank!" Some of the kids giggled, but I rolled my eyes. What a royal pain he could be, especially when we were discussing as serious a topic as Lincoln's ghost.

"Actually," Howard corrected, "at that moment in time, he had only been dead for around eighty years or so."

"Big difference!" Robbie said. "My feet stink by the end of one day!"

More kids began to titter, until Mr. Banner flashed them a scowl. "Children, let's stop acting like . . . children," he said. "Continue, Howard."

"It is even believed that Winston Churchill had an encounter with Lincoln's ghost while he was a guest in the Lincoln bedroom. And it is highly doubtful that a respected man like Churchill would fabricate such a story.

"During President Harry Truman's administration, his daughter, Margaret, often heard noises at night when she slept." Howard glanced up at me with a knowing expression. "But whenever she checked for the source of those noises, no one was there. When she complained about the disturbing sounds to her father, President Truman, he thought that the noises were coming from the settling of the floors. And so, he ordered the White House to be rebuilt. As it turned out, the architect told President Truman that the floors had been in near danger of collapsing. Some people believe that the ghost of Abraham Lincoln had come to warn Margaret Truman before anyone was hurt." Howard paused. "And that's the conclusion of my formal report."

It was like lights being flicked on suddenly after a great movie. We all wanted more!

"But I'd be happy to field any questions now," he said.

Almost every single hand went up.

Mr. Banner chuckled. "Howard, this is your crowd." He waved his hand in Howard's direction. "It's all yours."

Howard called on Carol Miller first.

"What about the times that people saw Lincoln's ghost in our school? Can you tell us more about those?"

"Certainly," Howard replied. "Other than the unexplained noises that Andi and I heard earlier this school year, there were two actual sightings of Lincoln's ghost in our school's history. The first one occurred back in 1938. At that time, Lincoln's ghost appeared to a sixth grader named Elias Morton. Lincoln was standing at the top of the steps leading to the auditorium, waving his hands in such a way that Elias felt he was telling him not to come any closer. A few minutes later, smoke was spotted coming from the auditorium, resulting in a major fire that caused most of the roof to be burned away and the attic and auditorium to be gutted. The next documented sighting was just a few years ago, in 1963, when another sixth grader, Janine Langendorfer, claimed to have seen Lincoln's ghost in the auditorium the day before President Kennedy was assassinated. Most of us still remember that shocking incident very well.

"Were both of those sightings a coincidence?" Howard propositioned. "I think not. I believe that the ghost of Abraham Lincoln appears at our school to warn us of impending events of doom."

I felt a chill run up my spine, all the way to the top of my head, and then back down again. Everyone was aghast at the prospect, talking in little groups or trying to ask Howard another question.

"Here, here, class!" Mr. Banner admonished. "I think that's a mighty big conjecture on your part," he said, turning toward Howard. "Let's stick to historical research with these reports, not our own interpretation of events. Those stories here at our school are just hearsay. The fact is children have active imaginations. It's highly questionable that either incident ever happened at all."

More hands flew into the air with questions. Howard called on me next.

"Other than the Margaret Truman incident, are there any other incidents you found in your research where witnesses have just heard—but not actually *seen*—Lincoln's ghost?"

"Yes!" Howard replied. "There have been many other incidents, not included in my report, where witnesses—many of them guests or employees at the White House—just reported *hearing* unusual sounds, like heavy footsteps, breathing, or knocking at the door, sounds like that. But then when they tried to find the source of the peculiar noises, no one was there."

I could almost hear the strange moaning tones that Howard and I had witnessed behind the curtain that day. Another chill tickled my spine.

That's when John Malone finally turned around to look at me. He was nodding and pantomiming words that I could not understand. I shrugged and shook my head. He pointed to his watch and mouthed the word "later," gesturing toward himself and then me.

My new resolution to hate John Malone went kaput. He wanted to talk with me after class! He hadn't forgotten about me after all! After class that day, John Malone and I would have a date, of sorts, even though I knew we had choir practice first. After class, John Malone and I would begin to hatch our clandestine plot to catch the ghost of Abraham Lincoln—*together*! My heart was thumping, bulging with love and anticipation, the adrenaline rushing through my body like a tidal wave. I turned to share my excitement with Keely—but only her empty desk stared back.

Chapter 12

As the rest of the class traipsed upstairs toward the auditorium for the final practice rehearsal before Friday's Christmas recital, John Malone was waiting for me under the stairwell. He pulled me back when I passed by, his finger to his lips.

"Listen," he murmured. "We've got to get a plan."

I nodded, but the ghost of Abraham Lincoln was just about the furthest thing from my mind at that moment. All I could think about was John Malone's touch on my sleeve and how brown his eyes were up close.

"You remember where I told you the ghost might be hiding, right?"

I nodded again.

"Then we just have to stake out and stalk him. The way I see it is, we only have one choice, and that is to sneak up to the auditorium after school and wait. I have a diagram and everything."

John reached into the breast pocket of the black CPO jacket he was wearing over his velveteen shirt. CPO jackets were the current rage for both boys and girls; Grandmom had promised she'd buy me one for Christmas. As he rummaged to find what he was looking for, a package of Winston cigarettes fell out and down to the floor. I looked at him, pretending not to be shocked, but apparently not doing a very convincing job.

He shrugged as if to say "no big deal," shoved the small cellophane package back into his pocket, and proceeded to explain the map to me as if nothing had happened. John's drawing was impressive, like an architect's blueprint. He had sketched a model of the auditorium down to the last detail, with every window, door, and space accounted for and neatly labeled. Pointing to the little room at the top of the spiral staircase, he said, "Here's the space we need to watch." Next, his finger slid over to a small area behind the wings of the stage facing the spiral staircase. "Here's where we can hide. It's a perfect spot. Then if we hear a noise in the space, we've got him. What'dya say?"

"Sounds like a good plan."

"Now, I'm not saying I believe that Lincoln's ghost is really up there," John said, his eyes traveling up toward the auditorium, "and I'm not saying that I really believe in ghosts . . . but something or someone is definitely hiding up there in that little space. I'm 100 percent certain of that. And I intend to find out who or what it is."

Mrs. Diggins suddenly called out to us from the top of the steps, and we peeked out to look at her. "You two again!" she shouted, digging her fingernails into her enormous hips. "Get up here—*now*! How rude! You expect us to hold up the whole practice waiting for the two of you to get good and ready to join us?"

"When?" I whispered to John, as we began climbing the steps toward the auditorium. Mrs. Diggins was huffing and puffing, but once she saw that we were heading in the right direction, she shook her head and returned to the auditorium.

"I figure we'll have to wait until after Christmas vacation," he said. "With this stupid recital, there are just too many people swarming around the auditorium after school these next couple days."

When we reached the top of the stairs, John hesitated before he pulled the door open. "Don't worry," he said. "If we really do see Lincoln's ghost, I'll let you talk to him first. I know that's important to you."

"But *how* do you know?" I asked.

He shrugged again. "When I came back to the bait shop the day I bought my hat, you and Ezra were deep in conversation. I didn't want to interrupt, so I kind of hid and overheard you. Sorry."

"That's okay," I said, beaming. I could feel my own eyelashes batting every bit as good as Roxanna Trixler's.

Two days later was the grand Christmas recital. There was no real school that day, just a big assembly with the entire school in attendance, beginning with several films on large movie reels, including my favorite, *The Littlest Angel*, and one with Jiminy Cricket retelling the Christmas story. It was difficult to hear some parts because I was sitting right beside the large movie projector, and the motor buzzed a constant grinding noise, not to mention the squeaking reels as each film neared its completion. Once the movie was finished and the top reel was empty, you could hear the flap-flap-flap of the film on the bottom reel until one of the teachers came to stop the projector, rewind the film, and thread the projector for the next movie.

In the afternoon, the actual recital began, starting with the kindergartners and then moving up. The grand finale was, of course, us—the sixth graders. By that time, many of the parents had arrived to see our performance, including Grandmom, who had somehow managed to hoodwink her way into a third-row seat.

Standing on the stage, dressed in our white tops and black pants and skirts, we began our stirring rendition of "God Rest Ye Merry Gentleman," warm under the surreal glow of the blue and yellow stage lights shining down on us, our voices reverberating. John's hair looked greenish in the odd light. He still wasn't singing. Against the spotlights' glare, Grandmom's face was a shadowy speck from my vantage point, but I could still sense that she had tears in her eyes. Mrs. Diggins's long fingernails were leading us like a baton, hypnotizing me. A feeling of warmth and well-being was enveloping me. I was convinced that John Malone finally liked me back. I thought about Keely. I thought about Ezra. I wondered if Abraham Lincoln's ghost was listening to our songs from his secret nest above the stage.

All of those distinct images and sounds swirled together like a vortex, taking me deeper and deeper inside of myself, until it became one of those transcendent moments that Ezra talked about—that strange state that you sometimes slip into when life seems to be standing completely still for an instant, long enough for you to catch it in your palm, like a snowflake, before it evaporates. Ezra said that those are the rare moments when we're in touch with our own eternal observer. "You have a heart and mind that are chronological," he explained, "but your soul is that ageless observer that lurks inside."

The moment lingered, magnifying the sensation. The stage lights overhead shifted into casts of red and blue, our shirts suddenly growing pink, our voices rising into the haunting harmonies of "Silent Night." I could feel my soul—not five years old, not eleven years old, not fifty years old, but somehow, all of them, all at once—peering out from a place so deep within me that I almost lost my breath.

PART 2

Chapter 13

Before Christmas vacation was spent, life ripened into a brand new year. Though the country was at war in Vietnam, and tension between the races was mounting in the bigger cities, the new year seemed, to me, rife with new hope and possibilities.

Grandmom and I stayed up late watching the Times Square celebration on television, huddled together under an afghan she had crocheted herself. Why thousands of people would travel all the way to New York just to cram into one spot was one of the mysteries of life Grandmom had never understood. Still, we watched, ticking off the seconds along with Dick Clark. 1967!

Later, I lay in bed counting the stars through my window, as I listened to the small pops and crackles from fireworks within our own neighborhood, embellishing my fantasies of what the new year might bring.

Two long weeks of vacation from school— fourteen late nights in a row—had given me ample opportunity to hone my daydreams to the finest detail. They always began with John Malone and me, sitting together in our little hideaway beyond the stage stalking Lincoln's ghost. It would turn out to be a longer process than anticipated, meaning we would continue our stakeout night after night after school, snug in our secret perch. In the process of spending hours together, talking and waiting, we would get to know one another in that special, intimate way that only certain situations allow, like soldiers in foxholes or neighbors sharing storm shelters.

Finally, one afternoon, John would confess. He liked me back, he would admit out loud. Next, he would smile at me and ask me to be his girlfriend. From then on, he would carry my book bag as we walked home from school, spend Saturday mornings sitting with me on Grandmom's front porch, and tease me on the playground while I played Bounce a Fly with the other girls.

One afternoon, our stakeout would pay off. From beyond the spiral staircase, we would hear peculiar noises and heavy footsteps, and then—voila!—the ghost of Abraham Lincoln would appear. At first, we would cower in fear, but not for long. Lincoln, we'd realize soon enough, was a kindly, gentle ghost. First off, he'd reassure me that there was definitely life after death. "And it's a wonderful life too," he would say in a booming voice befitting the ghost of Abraham Lincoln. Death, he would explain, is a shining city, with golden sidewalks and endless gardens, a place where all people and their pets—just like Pom Pom—retreat after they leave the earth, like an endless vacation spot. Abraham Lincoln would then reach out and caress my cheek, saying, "Your parents asked me to give you a special message. They wanted me to tell you that they love you very much, and that they are watching over you every day and always will be."

Afterward, John and I would become school heroes for our brave and historic accomplishment. This profound experience would, inevitably, bond us together for life. On the night of our high school prom, John Malone would ask me to marry him.

The long-anticipated third day of January finally arrived, and it was time to head back to school and begin living that happy fate I had conjured up—so rich and real in my mind that it seemed inevitable.

The first blessing of the New Year was that Keely had returned to school! As soon as I spotted her in the schoolyard that morning, I raced over and gave her a bear hug. "I'm so glad to see you!" I squealed. "I missed you so much!"

But she stepped back away from me, her whole body going stiff. Nodding, she said nothing in reply. I looked into her face. That's when I made the chilling discovery that Keely's eyes were *still* dead. They reminded me of the glass eyes of my old porcelain baby dolls. Her demeanor had changed too. She seemed more unkempt, somehow, though her blouse and miniskirt were clean and well pressed. Her hair was still styled in a flip, but the texture wasn't smooth like it had been before, more frayed at the ends. Instead of her usual stylish shoes, she was wearing tennis shoes and bobby socks, all wrong with a miniskirt. Even her mannerisms seemed less refined, almost heavy.

Keely had become a different person. Moving away from me and everyone else, she stood alone beneath one of the old oak trees, gazing around the schoolyard, awaiting the morning bell. I couldn't help but watch her, wondering what I could do or say to rouse her back to being my old friend. Then I saw her lifeless eyes hone in on someone.

It was Bertha Riggs, jumping up and down, belting out one of the newest Motown hits from WLS radio. As Bertha shifted her body, her gaze met Keely's.

I looked back and forth between the two of them. Keely continued to stare at her, not defiantly, but out of the numbness that she had become. Numbness was creepier than anger. Bertha must have thought so too because she diverted her eyes. I was hoping Bertha's surrender might be the cornerstone toward resurrecting the old Keely, but it seemed to give her no satisfaction whatsoever. Her empty eyes moved to another target, no intention in them, not even a twitch of a change in her facial expression.

As I tried to assimilate Keely's transmutation, another devastating sight caught my eyes. John and Roxanna Trixler were standing together near the front door, talking closely with that unmistakable body posture that only boyfriends and girlfriends share. What could have happened during the Christmas break? I felt my heart twist inside me, like an old wet washrag.

Roxanna looked radiant, wearing a shiny white coat with a white fur collar that she probably got for a Christmas gift. I was expecting John to grab her hand and hold it at any minute. Roxanna was chattering and chattering away, giggling all the while. Finally, her little pink mitten reached up and playfully punched him on his chest a couple of times.

John wasn't smiling, but he might as well have been. Instead, he was holding his chin up, fishing cap firmly in place, with the cocky look of a man who was showing off, smug in his ability to win the affection of the most beautiful girl at Lincoln Elementary School.

Sudden tears blurred my eyes. I wiped them away quickly before anyone could notice. But Alfreda already had. "He's not worth it," she whispered, slinging a comforting arm around my neck.

After school, I hurried to the bait shop, anxious to talk with Ezra. I hadn't seen him since the day of the fight. Not only did I miss him like crazy, but also it was a brand new month, meaning it was time for him to give me another reason that he believed in life after death.

As I reached the little shop, I stopped dead in my tracks. On the white shingles on the left side of the building, someone had spray-painted, in dark green paint, "NIGGER" in large, block letters in a vertical line. I couldn't imagine who would have done such a hateful thing.

Though I had been coming to Ezra in the hope of getting some consolation, I decided—this time—I would force myself to be strong enough to comfort *him.*

When I entered the shop, Ezra was standing amid a cluster of boys from my class that included Bernard, Howard, Kevin (the mulatto boy), John, and even Robbie Taggert. (Following our lead, Robbie was the only other white kid besides me and John who ever frequented the bait shop.) They were all talking at once, obviously hatching up some kind of scheme. Seth left his spot from among the group just long enough to greet me before returning to the manly huddle.

"We're gonna paint out the graffiti," Robbie explained to me, almost proudly. "That's what we're talking about now. We're making plans about when to do it."

I was impressed. "Can I help?"

"I don't see why not," Howard said. "The more, the better."

Ezra looked weary, his eyes troubled. "You kids are something else, you know that? There's only one problem."

"What's that?" John asked.

"You paint it out, they paint it back. That's the way it works around this neighborhood. If you're marked once, you're marked forever."

"But we can't just let it stay on there!" Keith said.

"When did it happen?" I asked.

"Over the Christmas holiday," Ezra said with a sigh. "Me and Seth went away for a few days to do some ice fishing, and when we got back, there it was."

"Who would do such an awful thing?" I asked.

Ezra shrugged. "I have my suspicions, but I can't be sure." He looked around at our forlorn faces. "Cheer up, kids. Things like this sometimes just happen. That's life." He mustered a smile, but I could tell he was as shaken up as the rest of us. Slowly, he left the group and moved over to the tall stool behind the cash register. Chin in hand, he began doodling on a sheet of paper.

"We can't just *leave it* on there," Keith repeated.

The group fell silent. Everyone was more than willing to help, but no one knew just what to do about it.

"Tell you what," Ezra finally said. "Let's try to make something nice out of it."

"Something nice?" John asked. "Like what?"

Ezra reached down to scratch the top of Seth's head. "Let's send them back a message, using their own. Let's let every letter of that word stand for something good!"

"What'you mean?" Bernard asked.

He motioned for us to gather around the front counter and held up the paper he had been scribbling on. On it, he had written the grisly letters that had disfigured his shop, in a long row, going down vertically, just like the vandals had sprayed them on the outside of his building. We all stared at the ugly word and then at Ezra. His fingertips were tapping his lips. He took the paper back and set it out in front of himself, again resting his chin in his palm. Finally, one at a time, beside each letter, he added more letters:

N   othing
I   n
G   od
G   ets
E   ternally
R   uined

"How's that?" he said, smiling and lifting up the paper again so that everyone could read it.

"That's cool!" Robbie said.

"So you saying we should add those words to each letter on the front of the building?" Bernard said.

"Yup. That's the plan," said Ezra. "What do you think?"

We could hardly wait to get started and probably would have run outside right there and then if Ezra hadn't calmed us down with some common-sense planning. "First of all, we don't have any paint yet," he said. "And we need brushes—and a design."

He assured us he would purchase a gallon of green paint the very next day, as close as he could find to matching the vandal's paint. "Now I want you all to practice your painting skills too so that you don't mess up my building any more than it already is," he teased.

We promised him that we would practice. That's when Howard had a brainstorm. In art class tomorrow, he told Ezra, we would inform Mr. Alphonse about our plans and solicit his expertise with the project.

The passionate Mr. Alphonse was only too glad to be of assistance. Not unexpectedly, he leaped up on top of a desk and literally saluted us, from one end of the room to the other, for our altruism in participating in such a worthwhile community project and for being all-around good Americans. "Hate is an awful, awful thing," he said. "And to take a message of hate and transform it into a message of love is, indeed, the essence of true art."

We spent the rest of the class practicing stencil lettering with a wide paintbrush. Mr. Alphonse told us that he would personally assist with the design, even supplying the brushes at no cost to Ezra. "In fact," he suggested, "we can make painting Ezra's shop our art class for Thursday. I'm going to call your Mr. Ezra right after school today and coordinate everything with him."

By the time Thursday rolled around, we had all the supplies that we needed. When it came time for art class, we marched over to the bait shop in two orderly, single-file lines behind Mr. Alphonse, who led us with the flair of a drum major, high stepping with arms flailing. The white kids who had never before traversed this side of Lincoln School trod cautiously over the cracked sidewalks, their eyes wide with anticipation. The black kids were just plain excited, anxious to take a stand in their own neighborhood (except for Keely, of course, her unchanging eyes staring blankly ahead as we approached the bait shop).

Ezra greeted us all with a large tray of Dixie cups filled with cherry Kool-Aid and two free pieces of candy for each of us. It moved me to watch Mr. Alphonse and Ezra shaking hands and exchanging their greetings and introductions. "Hey, man," Ezra smiled at him, "thanks for doing this with the kids." They looked like a poster for international peace or something, both of them so grandly good-looking, though polar opposites—Mr. Alphonse with his milky skin and wavy, blond hair and the exotic Ezra in his tunic shirt and long black dreadlocks.

We lined up to get our assignment. Some of us were to be paint stirrers, some the actual painters, some the cleaner-uppers, and some would just lend their moral support. Most everyone clamored for a job, especially the job of painter—but not Roxanna Trixler. She didn't want to risk ruining her new white coat. Her job, she grinned, would be to cheer John on from the sidelines. I felt like swiping a line of fresh paint across her smiling face but restrained myself for the cause.

What we didn't expect was that the local television station had somehow caught wind of our endeavor and arrived in a white van with "WSND" splattered across both sides. They wanted to film our art project for the evening news. Seeing the local anchor, Madelynn Maverick, and her cameraman really kicked things up a notch, prompting exceptional work (under the artistic mastery of Mr. Alphonse, who painted the actual lettering) and a lot of flamboyant antics as the boys vied to become the main focus of the camera lens, shoving each other around like first graders.

Madelynn Maverick stuck her microphone under Ezra's face, eager for a gratuitous comment. He seemed overwhelmed.

Mr. Alphonse rushed to his rescue with an eloquent statement about the kindness of our class responding to the kindness of Ezra, how life was a circle of karma where good begat good, and bad reaped its due in the end, including the abomination of the person who had vandalized Ezra's shop during, of all times, the Christmas season. "As you can see," Mr. Alphonse concluded, turning around and pointing to the work in progress with a sweeping gesture of his arm, "an ugly word is becoming a beautiful message about the transcendent power of love."

The finished product—completed in little less than one hour—was joyous, beyond all of our expectations. The left-side of Ezra's Bait Shop, with the transformed word, looked like a quaint storefront in some picturesque, faraway place like Greenwich Village in New York City or Haight-Ashbury in San Francisco—happy and bright, anointed with small painted flowers and little suns framing the new lettering. Luminous.

After school, I returned to Ezra's shop. By that time, he was sitting alone, not one customer in the store. He was counting out the day's receipts from behind the counter, supposedly, but I could tell that his mind wasn't on the task. His eyes, a smoky quartz color in the late afternoon light, drifted toward the window. His thoughts appeared to be a thousand miles away from the curling papers in front of him.

"Why would anyone do such an awful thing as vandalize your store that way?" I asked him.

The sound of my voice seemed to startle him out of his deep contemplation. "Got me, little girl," he said, shaking his head. "Emancipation was more than a hundred years ago. You'd think we'd have gotten much further along by this time, wouldn't you?"

It occurred to me then just how little I knew about Ezra. I guess he had always seemed more like someone who belonged to the universe, not to anything or anyone in particular. I decided to ask him about his family.

His face transmuted into an expression I had never seen before. It was lineless, yet the most melancholy expression I had ever seen. "My family?" He smiled weakly. "All of them have passed, I'm afraid. Except for Seth here, of course." He ruffled the dog's ears.

"*All* of them?" I was astonished.

"'Fraid so," he said.

"How did they die?"

"How did they die?" he repeated, his eyes drifting away from me, toward some image he was seeing in his mind. "My father, well, he was in the wrong place at the wrong time and was shot one night in Mississippi. That's where I'm originally from, you see. It all turned out to be a case of mistaken identity, but that doesn't matter much after they've already killed you, now does it? And my mother, well, she died of a broken heart less than a year later. I'm surprised she lasted that long, to tell you the truth; how she loved that old man."

"Who shot him?"

"A white policeman. He said my father looked too much like the other guy for his own good. And that was his defense. Everyone bought it. The jury thought that was a good enough reason for murdering the wrong person. And that was that."

I paused for a moment before asking, "Did you have brothers and sisters?"

"Just one older brother. He was a preacher. He had a lot of radical ideas inside of him. Good ideas, I mean. Just dangerous—ideas that were way too far ahead of their time."

"So what happened to him?"

"He was killed by an angry mob of white men who didn't care much for his ideas."

I didn't know what to say for a long time—it seemed like hours to me. Finally, words formed in my throat. "Ezra?" My voice seemed small, like it was coming from a vault deep inside of my chest.

"Yeah?" He was back to counting his receipts.

"Why don't you hate white people?" I asked.

He immediately stopped counting and looked me square in the eye. "Little girl, people is people, and you gotta take them just that way. One by one. You can't hate a whole group of people for something another person did, just because they're white. You don't hate all the blonde girls in your school just because of that little Jezebel who stole your John Malone, now do you?"

He had a point.

"Besides that," he continued, "hate is *never* an answer. It never solves a damn thing, and it never improves any situation. Hate is an energy-sucking black hole. If you remember anything I tell you, you remember that, okay?"

I paused again. "Did you ever have a wife, Ezra?"

He bit his bottom lip as if I had unearthed the deepest wound yet. His eyes slowly clouded over with tears, and his beautiful face, shrouded in sorrow, reminded me of the painting of Christ's face in Gethsemane that I'd seen hanging in Mrs. Baxter's living room.

"Sure did," he finally replied. "Her name was Lana, and she was the prettiest thing I'd ever laid my sorry eyes on. Pretty on the inside too. She died in childbirth. Took our baby girl right along with her."

I couldn't even move. It was as if a mist was filling the shop slowly, like smoke, and all the little bobbles, poles, and fishing thingamabobs were floating away in a foggy haze. I knew I needed to respond to him, somehow, in a way that was appropriate to the unbearable weight of the moment, but I was mute. If there were any words to say, I sensed I was too young to know them. All I could think of to do was to move toward him and, as softly as I could, wipe away the single tear flowing down his cheek.

"Ezra?" It seemed like the right time to ask. "Can you give me another reason that you believe there's life after death? It's a new month, you know."

"That it is, little girl, that it is." A smile beamed from the depth of his sadness, and it was glorious, like a rainbow. "What about injustice? Now that's a good reason. One of the best reasons to believe."

"Injustice?"

"Injustice. It would be impossible to explain all the injustice and inequality in this world if there was only one go-around, wouldn't it? There's gotta be something else, I'm convinced of that—a life or world beyond this one that makes some sense of it all."

Chapter 14

Grandmom really enjoyed watching our painting escapade on the six o'clock news. By the time the television editing crew had done its job, the segment was whittled down to less than one minute, all the action spliced together in quick, dizzying fragments. Grandmom kept pointing to the TV screen at all the bobbing kids in the background, asking, "Is *that* one you?"

But like Ezra said, people is people, and you gotta take them as they are, one by one. Not everybody relished the news story as much as Grandmom. Some of the white parents became downright outraged that Mr. Alphonse had, all on his own, sanctioned such a controversial art project—and on the *wrong* side of Lincoln School, no less. He had further sinned by not requesting signed parental permission slips to leave the school premises.

We could overhear the hubbub on our way to class the next morning. Principal Mortenson was standing in the hallway in the middle of a huddle of outraged parents. "But it was only one hour of the school day and two blocks away from the school!" he was saying. "Mr. Alphonse is one of our most popular and dedicated teachers!"

Later, he coalesced. The angry parents were right, of course, he eventually agreed. He would personally see to it that Mr. Alphonse was duly reprimanded. Carol Martin was only too glad to share the bitter turn of events with me.

This story also made the local news. Grandmom just about flipped when she switched on the television the following evening and there was Mrs. Miller, Carol's mother, hopping mad and wagging her finger in front of the camera. The next shot was of Principal Mortenson, sitting behind his gigantic mahogany desk, proclaiming that "appropriate disciplinary action" would be taken against Mr. Alphonse for neglecting to obtain proper parental consent slips for an outside field trip.

"You're all idiots!" Grandmom shouted at the TV.

Naturally, all of this upheaval carried over into the classroom for the next couple days, transforming it into a teeming den of resentment, with everybody choosing sides. There were three basic positions: those who clearly supported our art project, parents and all; those who sided with their angry parents and resented the excursion to the bait shop; and those who championed the project and were angry at their parents for being angry. Except for Keely, pretty much all of us had a clear opinion on the matter and knew where we stood.

Mr. Banner tried to settle us down, his eyes somber and apprehensive, reverting to that nervous, defeated look he had had at the beginning of the school year. At recess, two or three small groups actually came to physical blows before the teachers pulled them apart. The end result after all the commotion was that Mr. Alphonse was suspended for one week without pay.

People are people, to be taken one by one. Just like Ezra said.

Confrontation had forced Mrs. Henderson into an early retirement and eradicated Keely, but not Mr. Alphonse. Blue eyes blazing, he seemed to derive even greater energy and passion from his seven-day admonishment. His first day back to school, he sported a lavender necktie with yellow letters that said, "I think, therefore, I am." He explained it was a famous line from a philosopher by the name of Descartes. We couldn't really comprehend its precise relevance to the situation; nonetheless, we understood that it was his way of thumbing his nose at Principal Mortenson and the embittered white parents.

As January wound down, so did the romance between John and Roxanna Trixler. The final blow came when she tried to pass him a note one afternoon in class that got intercepted by Mr. Banner. Annoyed by the interruption caused by the errant note, Mr. Banner decided that her punishment, rather than a paddling, would be his reading the letter out loud.

"John," Mr. Banner read, his voice terse, "Why are you mad at me? Walk me home from school, and let's talk."

As the class giggled, Roxanna's face turned as red as the stripes on the American flag hanging over Mr. Banner's desk. John heaved an angry sigh, pushing the brim of his fishing hat downward to completely conceal his eyes.

And that was the end of them.

Oddly enough, Cupid's broken arrow did not give me the satisfaction I expected it would. Instead, it caused me new worries about John. Like Ezra had once hypothesized, something was not quite right about him.

Bernard had come close to becoming John's best friend when John had first transferred over to our school from St. Matthew's Catholic School. But as time wore on, they drifted apart, mostly because John had begun to pal around with another kid, for another short while. Robbie was on the verge of being his best buddy at the beginning of December, and then Kevin. Now he was hanging around with Howard on the playground.

Like it or not, I had to admit that Roxanna had been a sweet girlfriend to him—adoring, attentive, not pushy or anything. And yet, long before the confiscated note had cinched a bad ending between the two of them, John had been withdrawing from her too, bit by bit, a little more each day.

I was sensing a pattern. Maybe a person could only get so close to him before he started backing away. Maybe getting to know John Malone was like trying to catch a bubble. But why? The long bangs, the fishing hat—was he hiding behind them?

I glanced over at Keely, whose desk was still beside mine. I missed being able to mull things over with her. She was reading her science book. Whether or not she noticed from the corner of her eye that I was gazing at her, she didn't look up or acknowledge me in any way, not that I really expected her to. She never did anymore. She rarely spoke to anyone in class, except if it was absolutely necessary. I wondered if she blamed us for abetting Bertha's crime; like traitors, we had stood around and gawked rather than coming to her rescue. If I had tried to stop it myself instead of choosing to summon the nearest teacher, the fight might never have escalated to the point that it did. Maybe I *was* a traitor.

Loneliness was an elusive companion, like a butterfly that had visited me off and on since the day my parents had died, landing softly, at first, on my shoulder until I had a chance to realize it had returned. Then as soon as I got used to it being there, it flew away.

But it was back again.

Chapter 15

As soon as February 1 rolled around, I was at Ezra's door, awaiting his next reason to believe in the afterlife. Turns out, it was his best argument yet.

"If there isn't life beyond this one," Ezra said, "then all the great religious thinkers and all the prophets, throughout all of time, have been duped or deluded—from Jesus to the Pharaohs of Egypt, to Buddha, to Muhammad, to you name it. All the major religions believe in some sort of spirit or soul survival after this life. Do you think every single one of them could be wrong?"

It was a powerful explanation, difficult to refute.

One week later, it was my turn to deliver the oral report on Abraham Lincoln. After exhausting the ghost topic before Christmas break, we had moved onto the normal curriculum. Already, we had listened to reports on Lincoln's childhood, his prairie years, and his time as a young lawyer in Springfield, including the Lincoln-Douglas debates. We were just about to delve into the areas of his presidency and the Civil War. Mr. Banner informed us that these two topics were so vast and momentous that we would be studying them for the remainder of the school year.

This week's report, however—my assignment—was what Mr. Banner called a "wild card" topic where he drew names and allowed the chosen student to select any aspect about Lincoln's life for his or her oral essay. He threw in "wild card" assignments every now and then, just to shake things up and break the monotony.

"My oral report," I began, "is about how Abraham Lincoln's early life and experiences shaped the man he later became. Keely touched on this topic in her report. It was so interesting that I wanted to expand on it." It was a compelling opening statement, I had to admit. I looked at Keely, but her eyes were still flat and lifeless, as if she hadn't even caught the mention of her own name.

I wasn't one of the nervous kids who spent their entire oration just trying to steady the paper in their trembling hand, nor was I a flamboyant orator like Howard. Although I hovered somewhere in between the two extremes, I liked to fancy (as my second-grade teacher had once noted on my report card) that I had excellent expression when it came to reading out loud.

I looked at Mr. Banner to see if he was as impressed with the beginning of my essay as I'd hoped. He seemed to be, nodding his head and raising his eyebrows as he drummed a pencil on his desk. "Continue," he said.

"As we have already learned, Abraham Lincoln was born on February 12, 1809, in Kentucky in a little log cabin, with dirt packed down for a floor and one single window. He was born on a Sunday, and there was snow on the ground."

"It seems it was a day quite similar to today," Mr. Banner interjected as he gazed out through one of the large windows facing the barren oak trees in the schoolyard. "Today is February 8, and there's snow on the ground."

I didn't know whether I was annoyed with him for breaking my stride with the superfluous comment or spurred on because he was listening so intently to my every word. I decided to focus on the latter. "Anyway," I continued, "his father was kind of a drifter and moved around a lot. Lincoln's father moved his family, which consisted of Lincoln and his older sister, Sarah, and his wife, Nancy, to Indiana when Lincoln was seven.

"Abraham Lincoln adored his mother, Nancy Hanks Lincoln. She was said to be very pretty with sad eyes, tall and intelligent like Lincoln was, though she was uneducated. She was very religious. It was also rumored that she was an illegitimate child, which means that she was born out of wedlock."

As usual, some of the less mature kids snickered. Mr. Banner sat upright in his chair, a little startled, I guess, that I had decided to throw such a provocative tidbit into my report.

"That'll be quite enough," he scolded the gigglers. "Remember, Andi, rumors are just that: rumors. Continue."

"His mother encouraged Abraham's intelligence and his self-confidence," I read from my notes. "But not his father. His father, Thomas, didn't like him to read books. Lincoln was never close to his father. When Lincoln was nine years old, his mother died from milk sickness."

A hand immediately rose. "What's milk sickness?" Kathy O'Connor asked. Thinking no one would notice, she slipped a booger into her mouth with the index finger of her other hand.

But of course, someone always did notice. This time, it was Bertha Riggs. "Booger butt!" she exclaimed.

"It was a disease people got when they drank milk from cows who grazed on poisonous white snakeroot," I replied. "Anyway, it was a terrible time for Abraham Lincoln. When his mother realized she was going to die, she called him and his sister to her deathbed and instructed them to be good and kind people. Lincoln would always remember how he had to help carve the pegs for his own mother's coffin and how his father had hauled the coffin on a sled to a wooded hill and buried her there. Ten years later, Lincoln's sister Sarah died, and he felt all alone in the world.

"When Lincoln was just into his twenties, he witnessed a slave auction in New Orleans and was horrified by what he saw. Somewhere inside of him, he always believed that slavery was wrong.

"A few years later, when he was in New Salem, he became engaged to Ann Rutledge, who was his first true love." I looked up but tried to avoid looking directly at John Malone. From the corner of my eye, he seemed to be gazing out the window, toward the grove of oak trees on the lawn, still naked without their leaves. "But there was a lot of sickness going around that year," I continued, "and she died a few months later, in the summertime. Abraham Lincoln was devastated by her death, and his personality changed after that. He became so depressed, in fact, that his friends thought he might kill himself. They watched him closely.

"Later, he married Mary Todd, who was a very difficult woman. Two out of their four sons died during their childhood. All of these terrible losses, however, helped to make Abraham Lincoln the great man that he became. Because he had suffered so much, he could really feel the pain and suffering of other people." Although I was talking about Lincoln, my thoughts drifted to Ezra, the real inspiration behind my report. "In fact," I said, "I think that is the difference between great people and ordinary people. Great people have the ability to rise above the bad things that happen to them. They actually use their painful experiences as a way of understanding other people's pain. I think it develops inside of them almost like a sixth sense. They take this gift of seeing deeper inside of others, and they use it to make the world a better place.

"In Lincoln's case, he could feel the pain and suffering of the slaves. And so it was very important to him to free them, but also to help the North and the South come back together again."

There was only one question when I was finished, and it came from Roxanna Trixler. "What color was Ann Rutledge's hair?" she asked.

I honestly didn't know. Shrugging, I replied that it was probably blonde, but that was just a guess.

As the bell for recess sounded, and the rest of the class clamored to the door, Mr. Banner called me over to his desk. "It was a little more like a sermon than an oral history report," he said with a chuckle, "but you did an outstanding job, Andi. It was one of the most thoughtful reports we've heard all year."

By the time I arrived on the playground, John Malone was waiting for me.

"Hey," he said, pulling me away from Alfreda, out of her earshot, "I think it's time to put our plan in motion. How about tomorrow night, right after school?"

I thought he had long forgotten about our mission and was taken aback by his sudden, newfound intensity. I nodded but said nothing.

"After you finish your patrol duty on the first floor," he continued, taking my nod as tacit approval, "meet me at the bottom of the auditorium steps. Leave your patrol band on. That way, no one will bother you if they see you coming back up the steps. And don't tell *anyone*! You got it?"

"Not a soul," I said. "Cross my heart." I could see Alfreda standing in the background, flashing me a victory sign because John Malone had sought me out in such a clandestine manner.

"That means you don't tell Alfreda," he said. "Not even Ezra. This has to be top secret if it's gonna work."

The next school day, Thursday, was like an endless series of opening one book, then another, then another, and another. Even

Mr. Banner seemed to be teaching in slow motion, using meaningless words. Blah-blah-blah-blah-blah. The big round clock hanging near the transom above the door seemed stuck. Science class, in particular, droned on so slowly that I was nearly convinced the earth had come to a standstill.

But finally, three o'clock arrived—time for me to leave class, don my patrol girl's sash, and assume my post on the landing of the first-floor staircase, this week's assignment.

At 3:10 p.m., the dismissal bell clanged. Awaiting the heavy traffic that would soon begin pounding down the steps, I replayed John Malone's conversation in my head from the day before. I hoped I had all his instructions correct. I smiled when I realized that he had been watching me closely enough to know that this was my patrol post for the week.

"Walk! Don't run!" I heard myself saying to one of the fourth graders who was rushing down the steps at a dangerous pace. But it was a rote response. My mind was far, far away from patrol responsibilities, drifting upstairs two flights to where John Malone was waiting—for *me*.

Roxanna Trixler bounced down the steps next. She stopped in front of me. "I'll bet *you're* excited," she said. By the tone of her voice, I could tell she was either angry or making fun of me. How did she know? I wondered. After all that fuss about not telling a living soul, could John Malone really have spilled the beans to her, of all people?

"I saw John whispering to you on the playground yesterday," she continued. "Your little heart must have been pounding inside of you, wasn't it?"

I didn't say anything. Mostly, I was embarrassed that everyone seemed to know about my long-standing adoration of John Malone. Grandmom had warned me about the perils of wearing my heart on my sleeve. I wished I could be more mysterious, like Sophia Loren or Jacqueline Kennedy. No one ever knew what they were thinking until they granted a rare interview with *Life* or *Look* magazine. Grandmom said that, even then, they never really spilled their guts.

"Roxanna, you're blocking the flow of traffic," I finally said. "You'll have to move along."

She rolled her eyes. But when Bernard bumped into her from behind because she was standing in his way, she finally got the message and began descending the staircase with the rest of the kids.

After the big rush, a few more stragglers came down the steps, late because they had forgotten something or were detoured because they had to pee. The staircase was finally quiet. I glanced at my watch: 3:20 p.m.

Roxanna would laugh her head off if she knew how hard my little heart *was* pounding inside of me now, intensely enough to feel every beat as I mounted the steps, up toward the auditorium, where John Malone was expecting me. I wondered if this could technically be considered our first real date.

When he saw me, he kind of half-smiled, as if he wasn't certain that I would have enough nerve to go through with the stakeout. Then, his eyes darted around quickly; assuring that no one was lurking nearby as he pulled me underneath the stairwell. He opened a gray lunch pail. "I have a flashlight in here, just in case we need it," he said. "And I have an Instamatic camera and flash bulbs. I know they say ghosts don't show up on film, but I thought it was worth a try."

"You thought of everything," I gushed.

"You aren't planning to take your school books up there, are you?" he asked, observing my book bag.

I shrugged. "What am I supposed to do with them?"

"We can't have things weighing us down in case we need to make a quick getaway," he said. "I just left my books in my desk. Why do you take them home every night anyway?"

I felt myself blush. I was about to remind him that we had homework but decided against it.

"Just leave your bag here, under the steps," he advised. Before he could take it from me, I reached in and pulled out a paper and pencil to add to the supplies in his lunch box.

"What's that for?" he wondered.

"In case we see Abraham Lincoln, maybe I could get his autograph," I said.

John gave me an odd look but allowed my indulgence and clicked open his lunch pail so that I could drop the items into it. Then he shoved my school bag far back toward the wall, obscuring it behind a large silver trash barrel. "We'll come back for it on our way out of the auditorium."

I nodded.

"What time is it now?" he asked.

"Three twenty-five. What time do you think they lock the front doors?"

Not unexpectedly, he had already researched that part too. "I watched them a lot of nights, so that I would know exactly," he replied. "The janitor doesn't lock the school until around five o'clock. We've got little over an hour."

After one more quick scan, we moved out from the shadows of the stairwell and slowly, quietly, began climbing the slate steps up toward the auditorium. John stayed a few paces ahead of me, turning around every few seconds, his finger pushed against his lips to shush me.

The old door into the auditorium creaked as he pulled it open. He stopped. Opening the door just wide enough for us to sneak through, he allowed me to be the first one into the gigantic room.

The auditorium was dark, and I paused until my eyes adjusted. John did the same.

Because the space was also used as the gymnasium, the lacquered floor was difficult to walk across without making a sound. I could imagine the squeaking noises we might have caused if we had been wearing gym shoes and stepped just the wrong way. But we were wearing street shoes, John in his penny loafers and me in saddle shoes.

I walked behind him, tracing his steps. Finally, we reached the stage and mounted the three steps soundlessly. We slinked behind the velvet curtain, heavy with the smell of must and mold. I was imagining the next hour to come, the two of us holed up together in our little crawl space, whispering the secrets of our souls.

But it wasn't meant to be. Before we could even reach the tiny space, we heard noises coming from beyond the spiral staircase. John put his finger to his lips again as we listened. My heart started its erratic thumping again.

"Huh, huh, huh," came the sounds of very heavy breathing, obviously from a man, then a couple of moans, and then more heavy breathing. I cupped my fingers over my mouth to silence my own astonishment, my eyes wide, unblinking.

John was motioning me to move closer to the staircase, but just like the first time I had heard the noises with Howard, my legs felt like they were made of iron, fastened to the floor. C'mon, c'mon, John's impatient arm signaled.

Gathering my wits about me, I moved in close behind John. Slowly, as quietly as we possibly could, we began mounting the spiral, wrought-iron staircase. If he was afraid, which he must have been, he didn't show it in any visible way. My fingers were trembling as I grabbed the cold railing, but his hand was steady. We were moving slowly enough that I could count the steps. Ten more until we reached the closed door at the top.

The breathing became louder and more labored, followed by some sighs. It sounded like he was having a heart attack up there. Maybe Lincoln's ghost was dying, I thought quickly. Maybe we could be the ones to save him. Then I remembered that he was a ghost, already dead. Eight more steps.

John's pace seemed to be quickening, but maybe it was just my imagination. He was still wearing his fishing hat. If we had to make a quick getaway, I wondered if he would lose his hat in the process. Then everyone would know we had been up here. He should have thought of that in all his meticulous planning. Four more steps.

When John's foot reached the top step, he turned around to look at me, with both triumph and urgency in his eyes. Again, he pressed his finger to his lips. I nodded, moving in close so that we were side by side on the top step. Slowly, John pushed open the door at the top of the spiral staircase.

My mouth dropped open at the sight.

In that tiny space, Mr. Banner was seated on a chair still dressed in his suit coat, his trousers and underpants down around his ankles. Mr. Alphonse was kneeling in front of him, his head bobbing up and down.

Mr. Banner's eyes were half-closed, his head back, his tie loose around his neck. He was the one who was moaning and breathing hard, and he was making the same face a dog makes when you scratch him behind his ears. I couldn't even fathom what it was that I was seeing or what on earth it was that they were doing, but I knew it was something unmentionable.

"Gross!" John shrieked, a look of abhorrence on his face.

Mr. Banner's eyes popped open.

I think all of us gasped, or made some equally horrified noise, at that moment.

Mr. Alphonse turned around quickly to look at us, almost losing his balance. He had a strange look about him—his eyes were cloudy and unfocused, and his blond hair was disheveled, sticking up all over his head in spiky strands. Wearing only his shirt and suit coat, his bare back end loomed in front of us like a bright, full moon.

"Let's get out of here! Away from these queers!" John screamed, rushing passed me looking as if he was about to throw up. I followed right behind him, my thoughts so confused and contorted that I couldn't even think.

"Kids, wait!" Mr. Banner was hollering. "Come back! Let's talk!"

But it was too late. John paused at the bottom of the spiral staircase only long enough to vomit, and I moved around the mess just in time to avoid slipping on it. Together, we ran as fast as our legs would carry us, flinging ourselves past the velvet curtain, down the three steps from the stage, and across the squeaky gym floor that only minutes before we had inched across like night prowlers.

Chapter 16

Neither John nor I stopped running until we were safely outside of the school and down the front steps. When we reached the curb—our sides aching from the rapid, prolonged getaway—we stopped to catch our breath.

John looked ghastly. Still clutching the lunch pail, he was a greenish color, and his eyes had the hardened look of a man five times his age.

Even as we were racing down the staircases inside the school, the thought had occurred to me that we might start laughing once we stopped running, giggling hysterically and slapping our sides over the ridiculous scene we had just witnessed—not the least of which was glimpsing a teacher's bare butt!

But one look at John's tortured face, and I realized that something grave and unalterable had occurred. That's when I noticed his hat was missing.

"Are you okay" I asked. He looked as if he might puke again.

John raised his arm and slapped his hand through the air, waving both me and my question away from him, like an enormous gnat. "I'll see you later," he said in a taut, angry voice.

"But John," I cried. "I don't understand any of this! I need to talk!"

"Then talk to yourself," he said bitterly, turning away from me and walking away.

I must have stood there in front of the school for over half an hour before I could even move. I watched John fade away until he was a little speck that disappeared down a side street, toward his home. Part of me wanted to go back inside the school and hunt for his fishing hat. Maybe finding his hat for him would restore a modicum of normalcy and happiness—as happy as he got, anyway. The other half of me hated John Malone for abandoning me, for getting angry with me when none of this was my fault, for breaking my heart—again.

I suddenly remembered that my books were still stashed beneath the staircase. It seemed to make sense to go back inside and search for John's hat and my book bag. But I was too terrified to return inside the school. The prospect of encountering Mr. Banner or Mr. Alphonse was more terrifying than our original pursuit of Abraham Lincoln's ghost. What *were* they doing to each other up there behind the stage?

And then it dawned on me that Lincoln's ghost had never been beckoning to me, had never even been hiding in the auditorium at all. The sounds that Howard and I had heard way back at the beginning of the school year had been the two of them all along, Mr. Alphonse and Mr. Banner, doing peculiar things to each other without their pants on, month after month after school in their secret hideaway behind the stage. What *were* they doing to each other?

I wasn't so dumb that I didn't comprehend that there was something sexual about the whole thing. When I got my first period the previous summer, Grandmom had explained the whole thing to me. Though she had omitted the details as to exactly, precisely, how it all worked, I thought that sex was something that happened only between men and women. She had never told me that it was possible for one man to like another man in that way. If she had missed a whole big thing like that, I wondered what else she had left out.

The next time I looked at my watch, it was nearly 4:30 p.m., and my fingers and toes had numbed into ice blocks and were beginning to sting. I was surprised to feel frozen tears on my cheek. When had I been crying?

I began walking away from the school like a robot controlled by someone beyond myself. It came as no surprise, however, when the next thing I knew, I was knocking on the locked door of the bait shop.

The shop was already dark. But I didn't let that stop me. My pounding on the door over and over again roused Seth's booming bark, which finally brought Ezra out from his living quarters in the rear of the shop and back into the land of the fishing thingamabobs. When he saw me peeking through the front window, he unlocked the door. Seth barked a few more times before he realized it was me and then began alternately sniffing and licking me.

"What's the matter, little girl?" Ezra asked. "You look frozen to the bone. What you been doing—standing out in the cold since school let out?"

I scarcely knew where to begin. "I have a really big problem this time," I replied.

He led me over to the counter, took my gloves off, and laid them out on the heat register. My fingers stung even worse in the sudden warmth of the shop.

"Well," he said, sitting down on his stool, "let's talk about this problem of yours. The hardest part of any problem is admitting there *is* one. You already got the hardest part over with."

Taking my usual spot on the floor, I crossed my legs. Although the words came hard at first, eventually, I got the whole sordid story out—how John Malone and I were stalking Lincoln's ghost, our horror at discovering Mr. Banner and Mr. Alphonse at the top of the spiral staircase without their pants, how Mr. Banner called out after us but we ran away anyway, how John threw up, how cruel John was to me, everything.

Ezra listened without interrupting me once.

"I don't understand any of it," I concluded.

"It's a lot to understand," he said, blowing out a deep breath.

"John called them 'queers,' Mr. Alphonse and Mr. Banner. I don't understand what it was they were doing to each other. Do they love each other or something? Can men love each other like that? But Mr. Banner is married. He has a picture of his wife on his desk and everything, although she does look like an old sourpuss."

Ezra exhaled another deep breath, pursing his lips as if he was about to whistle, the face he always made when he seemed stumped to find just the right words to explain something. "Little girl, you ask some tough questions."

"I don't think I can look either one of them in the eyes ever again," I said. "I don't want them to be my teachers anymore, either one of them. I don't know exactly what it is they were doing to each other, but it was gross! I think that I should tell Principal Mortenson about them and what they were doing up there, don't you?"

For the first time since I'd known him, Ezra took out a cigarette from one of his pants pockets and lit it, almost ceremoniously, each step unfolding as if in slow motion—twirling the cigarette between his long fingers, striking the match, moving the match head to the tip of the cigarette, snapping the matchbook cover shut with one hand, then watching the smoke circle round and round over his head before he took even one puff. "You *could* do that," he said. "'Course, you and John had no business being up there in the first place, sneaking around and creeping up on people. But, you *could* tell on them. You sure could. And you're right—that was no way for teachers to act on school property. No sirree. Who knows, maybe they do love each other, but that's beside the point."

"It's just so yucky for them to have been naked in school, of all places! And teachers, of all people!"

"You're right." Ezra said. "They showed some poor judgment."

I nodded emphatically, crossing my arms.

"So, what do you think will happen when you tell your Principal Mortenson what you and John saw?"

I began playing the whole scene through in my head—requesting to see the principal, waiting in the secretary's office, and then finally being permitted to enter and sitting down in front of his enormous mahogany desk, his eyebrows knotted expectantly. "Well, Andrea," he would say, "what brings you into my office today?"

"Well, I guess he would be pretty mad at them," I said. "He might even fire them! . . . Do you think he really would fire them?"

"I think that's a pretty safe bet." Ezra blew a stream of smoke out of his nostrils.

"But they'd find another job, at another school, don't you think?"

"It's pretty doubtful. Once you get something like that on your record . . ."

"You mean they could never teach again?" I exclaimed.

He shrugged.

I was silent.

"And they sure would have a lot of explaining to do to their families, I imagine," he said. "The pain of that alone would punish them pretty good."

I remained mute. Mr. Banner was a wonderful teacher, quite possibly the best teacher I'd ever had. I couldn't live with myself if I was the cause of ending his career. And Mr. Alphonse—although he was an eccentric oddball, there was no doubt that he had a heart of gold and enough passion to fuel the entire school. They weren't really hurting anybody else, doing what they were doing up there. Ezra was right—John and I had staked them out and snuck up on them.

Then I thought about how it would be if the whole school found out about what John and I had seen. How all the kids would point at Mr. Banner and Mr. Alphonse and laugh at them, mock them, taunt them, call them "queers," just like John had. How all that humiliation and torment might drive them right out of the classroom, just like Mrs. Henderson. How their eyes might go completely dead after that.

And then I thought about Keely.

"I guess if I told on them," I said finally, "it would be kind of like what Bertha Riggs and the rest of us did to Keely, wouldn't it?"

Ezra didn't say anything, but he gave me a look that I'd never forget. His amber eyes were intense on mine, like he was gazing right through my eyeballs, straight into the depths of my brain matter. He seemed to be saying, with one look, that he was proud of me. Or maybe it was me who was just finally grasping a lot of the lessons he had been teaching all along—that people were complicated, not good or bad, but both at the same time; that we're all connected to each other deep down, part of the same giant heartbeat, and to hate or harm even one person breaks the chain.

Chapter 17

The next day was Friday. I set my alarm clock early that morning so that I could be the first one through the front doors of the school, the minute the janitor unlocked them. Grandmom wondered why I got up so early. I told her a half-truth—that I had left my book bag at school and needed to retrieve it before it got lost. She shrugged and started frying up the breakfast sausages, reminding me that she would be late coming home that night because it was Friday, her night to play bingo with the Catholic ladies.

Mr. Crenshaw, our custodian for as long as I could remember, was an amicable old black man with a gray mustache and salt and pepper hair—the tiny, curly gray hairs sprinkled together with the curly black hairs. He liked to rest his chin on the top of his push broom as the kids passed by and say weird things to them, like "if you don't pay attention, you'll wind up in detention."

He was surprised to see me standing outside. "Now whatchu doing here so early?" he asked. "You know you ain't supposed to be inside school before the bell."

"I have to come in," I explained. "I left my book bag here last night by mistake, and I need to find it before it gets lost."

Mr. Crenshaw shook his head and motioned for me to follow him. Together, we walked up the stairs until we were standing in front of his cleaning cart, where he carried all kinds of supplies—cleaners, sprays, buckets, and various sizes of brooms and mops. From underneath one of the ledges inside the cart, he retrieved my book bag. "This belong to you?" he asked.

I took it from his arms and smiled. "Thank you, Mr. Crenshaw!"

"Oh, you be most welcome, Miss Andi," he said. "Books, you see, they are very important. If you don't study, you ain't my buddy."

"Mr. Crenshaw?"

"Yup?"

"You didn't happen to find anything else unusual lying around, did you?"

He looked at me with a puzzled expression. "Like what?"

I took a deep breath and then decided to just get it out and over with. "Like a white hat? A fishing hat?"

"Sure 'nuff, I did," he said with a smile, pulling out John's hat from another one of the cubbyholes on his cart. "Now, I know this don't belong to *you*."

"But I know who it does belong to," I said, "and I promise I'll make sure that I give it back to him as soon as school starts."

"Belongs to that new boy, don't it? That one that looks like a little Beatle."

"John Malone?" I tried to say the name as nonchalantly as I could muster. "Yes, that's who the hat belongs to. He's in the same class I am, so I'll just return it to him today, save him the trouble of going to the Lost and Found."

Mr. Crenshaw eyed me suspiciously. "I'm not quite certain how your book bag ended up where I found it, Miss Andi, stashed under the stairs like that, like you was hidin' it. And then the little Beatle goes and loses his hat right nearby. Sounds to me like there might have been somethin' goin' on under them stairs that maybe shouldn't have been goin' on? How on earth your bag end up there anyway?"

I tried to think quickly. "Well, you might not know it, but I'm a patrol girl, and I left it at my post during patrol duty last night after school. Somebody probably just found my bag and stuck it there, under the stairs. That would be my guess, anyway."

Mr. Crenshaw stared at me for a while and then shook his head. "You dang kids," he said, "you tell more stories than the six o'clock news." He handed John's hat over to me with a sigh. "I ain't even gonna ask you how you knew that boy lost his hat. Just get yourself back outside before you get us both in trouble. And remember, if you break the rules, you'll both end up fools, y'hear?"

John Malone's fishing hat was nestled in the depths of my book bag. I couldn't get over the feeling. It was like capturing a piece of John himself. Part of me wanted to keep it and hold on to it, forever and ever. But the bigger part of me needed to return it to John—discreetly, of course—just to see the look on his face when his sacred old friend and protector was returned.

I waited for him in the schoolyard before the bell rang, but he wasn't to be found. Alfreda kept jabbering to me about some old movie that she and her grandmother had stayed up late to watch the night before. "I didn't get to bed until past midnight!" she said, and then she started going on and on about the convoluted plot again.

I kept nodding and asking questions, but all the while, I was keeping a watch-out for John. I was also fretting about seeing Mr. Banner. I couldn't look him in the eye; that much I was sure of. So I just wouldn't make eye contact with him ever again. I had it all planned out. I would scoot into my desk and go through the school day doing everything I was expected to do, except look right at him. It seemed the best plan I could come up with.

When the bell rang, I still hadn't seen John. I was getting apprehensive.

Instead of greeting us at the door like he usually did, Mr. Banner was sitting at his desk. I snuck a peek at him. He looked weary, deflated, like a balloon that had lost all its air. His posture was slumped.

Taking my seat, I stole another glance at him. Mr. Banner seemed to have the same plan as I did; he too would sneak a look at me and then turn away quickly. By the time the tardy bell rang, everyone was at their desks. Except John Malone. His ninth desk from the front, in the third row from the door, stood empty. It was a bad omen; my stomach twisted in knots.

I couldn't help but notice that Mr. Banner's eyes looked as worried as mine when he orally made the notation that John was absent.

The day began with a spelling test, usually my prize subject. Not having studied the night before, and with everything on my mind, I found I was unable to spell even half the words. Not only the tough words like "acknowledge," but also simple, stupid words like "bow"—for some reason I found myself stuck on even that one, as if the neurons in my brain had become disconnected or something. I couldn't put letters together. I ended up spelling it "bough."

I watched as Mr. Banner graded my paper first while we were silently reading pages 156 to 160 in our history books. Again, we locked eyes for a second, before I looked away. But when I moved my eyes back again, I could see him checking off word after word with his red pen. He looked up at me then with the saddest expression. This time I didn't divert my eyes, nor he his. Crumpling my spelling quiz, he threw my paper in the trashcan beneath his desk.

At recess, it was more of the same thing. When I told her I didn't feel like playing Bounce a Fly with our usual group, Alfreda opted out of the game too. Instead, we stood by the corner of the wire fence that enclosed the playground and talked. Or she talked, and I listened.

"What's the matter with you?" she finally asked. I told her I had a stomachache, that's all.

Recess was nearly over when I spotted John Malone strolling toward the playground from the other end of the schoolyard. It was odd to see him without his hat. I noticed he was walking kind of funny, almost shuffling, and nearly stumbling a couple of times. I could hardly contain my relief at the sight of him.

The bell rang, signaling the end of recess. The kids began accumulating from all corners of the playground into three single-file lines by the back door. I raced to the line to be nearer to John.

To my surprise, he seemed to be looking for me too, squinting and scanning the line face-by-face. Once he had ferreted me out from the group, he cut in line right behind me, in front of Carol Miller, who gave him a dirty look.

John moved close to me. "Don't even *think* about telling anyone," he whispered. "No one will believe you, and it'll only make things worse." His breath smelled terrible, a little like Grandmom's Geritol. I wanted to ask him if he was okay, but I remembered how angry the question had made him the night before, so I held my tongue and nodded in agreement.

"You cut!" Carol Miller snapped at him. "I'm telling!"

"Oh, shut up," John said. "All you ever do is whine!" The comment further infuriated her.

"Mr. Banner!" she screamed. "John cut in front of me! Mr. Banner!" Mr. Banner looked up and began walking toward us. Smug that she had been able to summon his attention, she delivered one final dig to John. "And you stink too! What *is* that smell?"

Mr. Banner stopped in front of us. "*John!*" he said, relief in his voice, not one trace of anger.

"John cut in front of me!"

"Oh, give it a rest, Carol," Mr. Banner replied and then seemed to snap back into his more teacher-like self. "Let's just let it go this time, okay, Carol? We'll all get back into school eventually, whether we're first in line or last."

She frowned. "And he stinks too!"

"So I've noticed," Mr. Banner said softly, almost to himself. Returning his attention to the group at-large, he commanded the lines to begin moving inside the school. John said nothing to me as we trotted up the stairs. By the time we reached the second floor, Mr. Banner was already standing outside the door to our classroom. As we passed by, he motioned for John to step out of line, saying, "I'd like to have a word with you." Almost as if it was an afterthought, his hand grazed my shoulder. "You, too, Andi."

John rolled his eyes. I thought that he might bolt, but he didn't. Instead, he kicked at the floor restlessly with his shoe.

"Just wait for me here, kids," Mr. Banner said. "I'll be back to talk to you in just one minute."

Stepping inside the classroom, John and I listened as Mr. Banner instructed the class to open their books and begin reading pages 230-240 in our science book. "And read it good because we'll have a quiz on these pages right after that."

"*Ten* pages?" Robbie moaned.

"Just start reading!" Mr. Banner snapped. "And the first one who talks is getting a paddling."

Closing the door behind him, he rejoined us in the hallway.

John stamped his toe against the floor and looked up at him. "I don't really care what the hell you have to say to us. There's not one word you *can* say that will change anything."

Mr. Banner nodded. "I understand, John. And I apologize for what you kids encountered last night. I know it looked rather peculiar, but it's something very private that you should never have been a witness to. I'm just so sorry. So very, very sorry. I don't really have any explanation that you'd be able to understand—until you're much older."

"Gee, let me take a wild guess what the two of you were doing," John said, laughing. "Maybe you were practicing for a play up there behind the stage—The Queers of Lincoln School!"

Mr. Banner looked as if John had sliced him with something sharp, right through the heart. For a moment, I thought he might even cry. "John," he said, his voice quivering, "I can smell that you've been drinking."

I went from being stunned to mortified.

"How much alcohol have you drunk?" Mr. Banner asked.

John's eyes looked glazed over. He shrugged. "Not enough to believe anything else that you have to say—ever again."

"Given the circumstances," Mr. Banner continued, "I think you should just go home and sleep it off. We'll talk later when your mind is clear. I'm not going to say anything about this to anyone. Just go home before any of the other teachers see you. But we *will* talk later. Do you think you can get home okay?"

"You're saving your own skin more than mine," John seethed before turning around and walking away from us. Grabbing the railing, he plunged down the staircase in a strange, clumsy way, stomping wildly as if the steps were moving objects.

When I looked up at Mr. Banner, his eyes were filled with tears.

Chapter 18

Everything was wrong.

John Malone was drunk. Mr. Banner was so depressed that he could hardly raise his voice loud enough to teach. Mr. Alphonse, we learned later that day, had taken it upon himself to resign, informing Principal Mortenson that a personal emergency had arisen that demanded his immediate, extended attention (but I knew his real reason was to protect Mr. Banner). The old Keely was long gone, not likely to return. And Abraham Lincoln's ghost had never been anything more than a figment of my lame imagination, meaning the possibility of life after death seemed more remote than ever.

The world, my world, was spinning out of control.

The only saving grace seemed to be, for some odd reason, John Malone's fishing hat stuffed in the bottom of my book bag. Maybe I was deceiving myself, but something inside kept telling me that returning the magical hat to him would somehow make things better for all of us—or at least make things better for him.

After seeing him drunk that morning, I spent the rest of the school day musing how to return his hat to him. I even considered visiting his house after school, where, presumably, he was sleeping it off as Mr. Banner had instructed. But I didn't know what time his mother came home from work from her job as secretary at the Bowington Factory, and I didn't want to risk meeting up with her and jeopardizing John's confidential condition. His father, from what I understood, worked long hours, rarely arriving home before John was in bed.

What was John doing now? I kept picturing him, all alone in the house, sneaking into his father's liquor cabinet, getting drunker and drunker by the minute, lighting up Winston cigarettes, one right after another.

John Malone was the oldest twelve-year-old I could imagine.

Even Ezra was not himself. As I helped him close up his shop after school that Friday, he seemed—for the first time ever—anxious to get rid of me. Ten minutes early, he had turned the "open" sign hanging in the door, over to the "gone fishing" side, explaining only that he was tired. He looked exhausted. And pensive. And preoccupied.

He kept saying things to hurry me along. While I swept the floor, he said, "That's enough, Andi. The floor looks clean enough to eat off of. Just stop now." When I offered to wrap the coins in the paper rolls, he declined, explaining that he hadn't accumulated enough loose change that week to make the project worth my effort. Dejected, I finally surrendered and headed for the door.

"You have a nice weekend, little girl," he called out after me. I turned back and saw no beautiful smile, like usual. His eyes were focused on the clock.

Grabbing the doorknob, I was soon outside in the cold. Two white men were standing across the street from the bait shop, rough-looking characters in my estimation, dressed in black leather jackets and smoking. With angry, frowning expressions, they both glanced over at me when I emerged from the bait shop. I might have been afraid if they hadn't broken eye contact with me as soon as they spotted me and turned their backs the other way. Still, I rushed in the direction toward home.

I stopped in my tracks when I reached the end of the block. Something felt wrong. In the first place, Ezra hadn't locked the door behind me, the first thing he always did whenever I was the last one to leave the shop. Besides eyeing the clock every few seconds, he had been pacing near the rear of the bait shop, back where his living quarters began, totally oblivious to the front door as I left.

I was fighting with myself; instinct was telling me that I should go back to him. But as anxious as he was to get rid of me, I didn't want to risk annoying him. I took another step closer to my home, further away from Ezra, and then stopped again. The open door was bothering me, and so was the sight of those two men across the street. The vandals who had sprayed the shop with graffiti during Christmas had never been identified.

Turning around, still fixed in the same spot on the sidewalk, I stared at the bait shop. Finally, I came up with a reasonable compromise: I would go back to Ezra just long enough to remind him to lock the front door and alert him to the two men. Then I would be on my way. What could be the harm in that?

The men were still there, standing in the same spot across the street, when I returned. Pulling the front door open slowly, I tried not to rouse the bells and frighten Ezra with my sudden return. Seth was still lying in his special spot under the counter by the heater where a beam of late afternoon sun was warming the hardwood floor beneath him. He rushed over to greet me. Ezra was nowhere to be seen.

I was just about to call out his name when I heard talking, just beyond the door, slightly ajar, leading into his private living quarters. Immediately, I recognized the other voice as John Malone's! Ezra was asking him if he was feeling any better, and John replied that he felt okay, except for a bad headache.

"I wouldn't doubt it," Ezra said. "That stuff'll kill you or at least make you wish you were dead. No more throwing up?"

"Nah."

Now I was in a quandary. Since they were talking in Ezra's house, where I'd never been before, not the bait shop, I knew it had to be a very private conversation. None of us kids, as far as I knew, had ever been allowed inside Ezra's private home. Besides that, Ezra had not given me one indication that afternoon that John Malone had been hiding in his house all along. What could he possibly be doing there? I didn't want to be an eavesdropper; Grandmom always told me that eavesdropping was akin to stealing, worse than stealing, because eavesdropping robbed a person of something much more precious than possessions.

And yet, there were other considerations far more serious to contend with. Ezra's front door was still wide open, and only he had the key to lock it from the inside, hanging on a silver chain that he kept in his pants pocket along with a pocket watch. What if somebody else—like those two shady characters outside—wandered into the bait shop, intending to do harm to Ezra? What if someone else wandered in and overheard them—someone who could not be trusted?

"Drinking is not the answer, John," I could hear Ezra saying.

As long as I remained, I could be the decoy. If an intruder appeared, I'd give out a shout to warn them. Besides that, given the intimacy of the moment, it did seem an opportune time to wait around and return John's hat to him when they had completed their secret conversation. I could sneak out and wait for John outside the bait shop. As soon as I spotted him, *bam!* There I would be—handing him back his hat without one eyewitness. When else would I have the opportunity to be with John in such complete and utter privacy?

"You ready to talk, boy?" Ezra said. "Your head clear enough to tell me what's going on?"

Finally, there was one more reason to remain—the most compelling one of all—though there was nothing noble about it: my own overpowering curiosity. I didn't have the strength to force myself *not* to listen; I had too much at stake to turn back now. And so I squatted on the floor beside Seth, behind the counter.

"I'm really glad you chose to come here to sleep it off, instead of going home to an empty house," Ezra said, "but you gotta talk to your parents about this."

"A lot of good that would do," John said.

"Why you say that?"

John's next words were mumbled, and I could not understand them. Ezra began coaxing him to come clean, to spill the beans about what was bothering him. "I know what you and Andi saw the other night with your teachers," he said. "Is that what's on your mind now?"

"Not really," John said. Then he started mumbling again. All I could pick up through the half-open door was the low, defiant cadence of his voice until, finally, there was only silence.

"John Malone, I give up," Ezra said with a sigh. "I just can't figure out why you're such a tormented kid. Don't you know that confession is good for the soul?"

That struck a nerve. "The hell it is!" John yelled, loud enough to perk up Seth's ears. "Confession is the biggest joke of all! The priest is the one who needs to confess his sins, but fat chance that'll ever happen! Dirty, scummy pervert!"

"John, what on earth are you talking about?" Ezra said. "Tell me, boy. Just get it off your chest, whatever it is that's got you so tortured. It's gonna be all right."

Seth's ear relaxed; he stretched out his front paws. My own legs were falling asleep, so I stretched them out from under me and settled into a more comfortable position, my back resting against the wall. As I crouched there on the hardwood floor, the next sound I heard was John's voice. Finally, the long-kept secret of John Malone began to unravel.

"Father Bob, the priest at St. Matthew's and the school principal, was always a weird guy," he began. "He even looked creepy with his cold, bulgy eyes and wormy lips. He reminded us of a dead fish . . . Anyway, when I got into the fifth grade at St. Matthew's, I found out that he was taking some of the boys in my class—and the sixth-grade class too—into the locker room after gym class, one by one. He told them that he had to do hernia checks on them."

He paused for a moment before continuing. "I thought that it sounded freaky right from the start, because he only checked some boys and not others. But he said that it was all part of his job and that, with his years of experience, he could tell which boys were more likely to develop hernias than others.

"One time during the fifth grade, it was my best friend's turn. Roger and I knew each other since we were little kids. I remember the day Father Bob first called him into the locker room and closed the door. But it didn't seem like that big a deal at the time, since we all knew it was just something Father Bob did. Just like a doctor. After a while though, Roger changed. He wasn't the same kid. I couldn't figure out what happened to him. He started crying a lot, like he was turning back into a little kid or something. He even started to suck his thumb when he got upset and thought no one was watching. But the other kids noticed and made fun of him.

"It wasn't until we started the sixth grade that he told me what Father Bob was really up to. He said that it all started out kind of normal, like a real hernia check, but after that, Father Bob told him he was really special and asked him to be his secret assistant. He told him not to tell the other kids because they would be jealous of him and start picking on him even more. That's when he started to do disgusting things to Roger when they were alone, not only in the locker room, but also in the rectory and in the boy's bathroom. He even fooled around with him in Roger's own bedroom when he came over to have dinner with his parents, offering to help them out by saying nighttime prayers with Roger and tucking him into bed. He told me that Father Bob would force him on his lap and command him to recite the Lord's Prayer while he fiddled around with him. He'd make Roger do all kinds of gross things to him too.

"I hated Father Bob's guts after that and started smarting off to him. He would whack me around and call me a sinner because of my 'rebellious spirit.' He said I was going straight to hell if I didn't shape up. He even called my parents into school for a conference and told them how concerned he was about me.

"I didn't say anything because Roger made me promise that I wouldn't tell another soul. He told me that Father Bob threatened to kill himself if he ever told, and Roger was convinced he would rot in hell if he had the death of a priest hanging over his head. Besides, Father Bob was the principal; who was I going to report him to? So I didn't know how I was going to do it, but I knew I was gonna catch that creep in the act and teach him a lesson before he ruined any more kids. Once I got the proof, I wouldn't be afraid to tell on him."

"Sure enough, one day in gym class after I was smarting off again, he informed me that he wanted to do a hernia check on me after class. When we were alone, he got nice all of a sudden. He said that I shouldn't act like such a wise guy all the time because he thought I had real potential. He offered to work with me, in private, to help me improve my attitude. He said that after he tutored me, the change in me would really make my parents happy and proud—that I owed it to them, and to God even more, to be a good boy. I knew he was trying to set me up.

"But it was the chance I'd been waiting for. All the time that he was talking, I was making my plan. When he walked away for a few minutes to find his rubber exam gloves, I grabbed a big wooden crucifix off the wall and slid it behind me, on the chair. He came back with his glove already on and kneeled down in front of me, a repulsive expression on his face like he was half sleepy and half excited. Then he pulled his glove off, smiled at me, and told me I was a very handsome boy. The minute his slimy fingers began stroking me in a way that I knew was no hernia check, I reached behind me for the crucifix and shoved it into his chest hard enough for him to fall backward on the floor. He was having a hard time getting up because of his long skirt, which gave me a chance to sock him in the eye. Then I kicked him straight in the balls as hard as I could. One of the other priests heard him yelping like a little girl and ran into the locker room.

"I told on him to the other priest, and I told my parents. But nobody believed me. I begged Roger to come clean and share his story too, for both our sakes, but he was furious with me and told me he'd deny everything if I ratted on him. Father Bob, of course, put on his pious act and told my parents that he would pray for my forgiveness. Then he expelled me from school—and church too, if you can really do that. I guess his black eye swelled up pretty bad, and explaining it to people was a big embarrassment. My parents stopped going to church too, and they'd been going to St. Matthew's for as long as I can remember. They were married there. By Father Bob. They couldn't believe I was so evil that I would beat up a holy Roman Catholic priest. They said I must be straight from the devil to make up such awful lies about him.

"That's when I learned that you can't trust anyone."

Ezra finally spoke. "John, listen to me, boy. *I* believe you. I believe every single word you've told me today. And not only do I think that you're *not* a bad kid; I think you're an almighty hero."

Next came a sound that I never thought I would hear: John Malone began sobbing. More than crying, he was nearly shrieking from pent-up sorrow.

Chapter 19

Ezra was comforting John, his voice low and soothing, the way it always got when he gave solace, soft as a pillow, secure as a safety net. "It's gonna be all right, boy," he was saying. "It's gonna be all right."

John's sobs seemed to go on forever, long enough to seem as if there would never be another sound ever again. Finally, he stopped crying, and there was only silence for another long while.

"So what about that fishing trip, soon as school lets out?" Ezra said. Though I could not hear John's reply, I assumed it to be a nod of his head, judging by Ezra's next remarks. "Good, good, then," Ezra said. "We'll have us a good time. Get away from here, go fishing with old Carter and the others. You know, a fisherman is a special kind of breed, don't you? And there's nothing better for what ails you than spending time with the river."

"Why's that?" John asked.

"Because the river's been around forever, young John," Ezra said. "Seen it all. Lived through it all. Still, it goes on and on and on. Not like our nonsense. We're only here for a blip of time, acting the fools most of it. But the river? Man, the river knows secrets. The river knows eternity. Yes, indeed. Old Man River is a great teacher if we sit still long enough to listen to him."

Next, I could hear kitchen sounds, the rattling and clanking of pots and pans, which was enough to rouse Seth from my side and join them. Their voices were muffled, but I could hear enough to discern that Ezra was preparing John a meal. "Bread will soothe your stomach," I heard Ezra say.

How I longed to be there with them, sharing food and conversation, but more than that, the chance to be with—besides Grandmom—the two people I loved most in the entire world, in such an intimate setting as a warm kitchen on a Friday evening.

I suddenly remembered my own presence again. It was almost as if I had become invisible, even to myself. Suddenly, there I was again, still sitting on the floor behind the counter, an intruder hiding in the dark. It was getting late, going on five-thirty. Grandmom would be home from bingo in less than an hour. I stood up to stretch my legs and peeked out the window. The two scary men were long gone. I inched closer to the door of Ezra's living quarters.

He was asking John's permission to telephone Mr. Banner.

"What's the point?" John said.

Ezra explained that he would advocate on his behalf with Mr. Banner, who he hoped might then arrange a conference with John's parents to help them better understand the truth about Father Bob. With two adults on his side, Ezra said, maybe they might come around to believing John's version of the story.

"Do what you want," John said, "but I already told my parents everything that happened. Besides, they'll probably get even madder at me if they find out I told *you*. They were pretty clear that they never wanted to hear anything about it ever again—or have me tell anyone else about it either. Besides—sorry, Ezra—the fact that you're black will probably bug them most of all."

They were silent for a few seconds, and I was imagining the expression on Ezra's face, the way his eyes changed the second he stopped smiling, like the sun blotted out by a passing cloud.

After a while, the happy noises resumed—the clanking of empty dinner dishes, the freezer opening (I imagined that Ezra was probably dishing out ice cream for the two of them), a contented dog's tongue lapping up a bowl of food, and even some laughter from John Malone. Finally, I could hear the wrapping-up sounds of both of them calling it a day. I thought about waiting outside and returning John's hat as I had originally planned, but the moment no longer seemed appropriate.

I quietly crept back to my place behind the counter and peeked out as John was leaving Ezra's private living quarters. Though I caught only a few seconds' glimpse, I was amazed by the look on his face, his brown eyes teeming with newfound aliveness, as if a spotlight had been flicked on inside of him. It was the first time I had ever seen him without the least bit of tension, no little lines creasing his skin, no bent head scanning the world with distrust. I was convinced that I was witnessing the quintessence of John Malone's wondrous face, so flawless that it nearly took my breath away.

The bells clanged as he slammed the door and left the bait shop.

Ezra was already on the phone, asking if he had reached the Mr. Banner who was a teacher at Lincoln Elementary School. After several long minutes, I heard him say, "Mr. Banner? Yeah, man, really glad I found you. My name is Ezra Thompkins, and I own the bait shop down the street from the school, and I really need to talk to you about one of your students, John Malone." Then he repeated John's tale about Father Bob and how no one—not his parents, his church, or his school—believed his story. He was quiet for a time after that, presumably listening to Mr. Banner's response. "I know it's hard to believe a priest could do something that horrible to a kid, but I believe him. Where would he come up with a story like that?"

Ezra was silent again for several more minutes as he listened to what Mr. Banner was saying. "People use alcohol when they feel trapped," he said, "and who feels more powerless than this poor kid? . . . Look, man," he said finally, "I know all about this thing with you and Mr. Alphonse, and we both know this is a completely different kind of situation. It just confused the poor kid even more, but we'll get that straightened out . . ."

It was difficult being privy to only one side of such a complicated conversation. Mr. Banner's response seemed to be sympathetic, gauging by Ezra's next series of comments, a lot of "you bets," "sure things," and "you got that rights." At one point, however, Ezra became angry. "That's a bunch of bullshit!" he shouted through the receiver. "Kids *aren't* resilient! Kids just know how to stuff their pain, way down deep. Then they spend the rest of their lives fighting to keep it from rising to the surface. That's not what we want to happen to this kid, is it?"

By that time, the hour had grown too late, and it was already dark. I decided to come clean. As soon as Ezra was off the phone, I quietly crept out from under the counter and knocked softly on the door to his private quarters, still left wide open from John's departure.

"Ezra?" I said softly. "I'm sorry, but you forgot to lock the bait shop door when I left. I was scared for you, so I came back to tell you. Anyway, I heard the whole thing."

His eyes rolled toward the ceiling in a look of utter surrender, and he let out a sigh. "You kids are gonna be the death of me yet."

Chapter 20

Before I left Ezra's shop that evening, he made me cross-my-heart promise him two things: that I would never repeat John's story to anyone and that I wouldn't confuse what Father Bob had done to Roger with the Mr. Banner and Mr. Alphonse episode. Though both of us were too exhausted by that time for another in-depth conversation, Ezra convinced me that it was too grown-up of a topic to explain to me in a way I could comprehend just yet, but to just trust him, for now, that what he said was the truth. Then he walked me part of the way home, stopping just shy of the white side of Lincoln School.

I was never made privy to the plan that he and Mr. Banner came up with on the phone that evening, but a few days later, as I was finishing my patrol duties, I was surprised to see Ezra coming up the stairs toward our classroom, dressed in a snazzy brown suit and a gold necktie, his long dreadlocks tied respectfully into one thick bundle at the nape of his neck. He wouldn't tell me just what he was doing at school, but seconds later, Mr. Banner rushed out and ushered him into his classroom, along with a middle-aged couple that I surmised to be John's parents. The woman's haggard eyes resembled John's. Her mannerisms were skittish; every few seconds, she was jerking, twitching, or tugging something back into its place. His father, on the other hand, looked defiant, impenetrable, as if every emotion, nerve, and muscle inside of him was manacled and shackled. (John had shared with us once that his father had been a decorated soldier during World War II and that his father had given John his middle name "MacArthur" out of his admiration for General Douglas MacArthur.) Mr. Banner led them all into our classroom and closed the door behind him. I wondered if John knew about the conference.

Whether it did any good, I didn't know. But I assumed the discussion had not gone well because the next day, John's bangs had been sheared haphazardly by his father again, and he refused to make eye contact with anyone. How I longed to give him back his fishing hat right there and then, so that he could pull it over his forehead and press his bangs down longer, but I didn't dare attempt such a blatant thing in the light of day and risk making things even worse for him.

After that conference, John had his good days, and he had his bad days. Some days, he came close to smiling, sometimes even at me. Other days, he disappeared inside himself or rolled his eyes whenever he caught me staring at him. But at least, he never came back to school drunk ever again.

Later, I would come to discover that something major had changed. Though John still came to see Ezra every day in the bait shop after school, one day I overheard him telling Bernard to never let his parents know he was still visiting the bait shop. When Bernard asked him how come, John shrugged and replied, "They kind of hate Ezra's guts."

Something else happened too, not much later. One afternoon when I arrived at the bait shop, it was closed. It was odd that Ezra had closed the shop during business hours; I'd never known him to do such a thing. I sat on the stoop and waited for half an hour for him to return. When he finally did, he was wearing his brown suit again, this time with a black necktie. He was holding some literature in his hand, a program with a picture of St. Matthew's Church emblazoned on its cover.

My jaw dropped open at the sight. "Did you go to talk to *Father Bob*?"

"Don't even go there, little girl," Ezra said. As he spoke, he waved his hand as if slashing the air, his eyes blazing. After that, he tore the literature in half and threw it to the ground and then kicked the side of the front stoop so hard that I thought he might have broken his toe. A little white card fluttered to the pavement in the process. When I picked it up to hand it back to him, I saw that it was like a business card, with the name and phone number of the bishop of the archdiocese printed on it. I knew better than to ask any more questions.

Now it was the middle of April. Two long months had gone by, and I still had John's fishing hat at the bottom of my book bag. I kept waiting for the right time to give it back to him, but it never seemed to come to fruition, for one reason or another, mostly because someone was always around.

Besides that, selfishly, I had grown to love possessing the hat that had provided him such comfort and strength. Maybe it really *was* a magic hat. During the school day, I would reach down into my book bag and stroke the soft canvas material with my fingertips, reveling in my secret capture of a piece of John Malone. At night, sometimes I would take it out and just look at it, enraptured to have the essence of John Malone with me in the sanctity of my own bedroom. The sight of it and the feel of it in my hands never ceased to fill me with a wondrous kind of joy.

About the only good thing that happened during those two months was that the old Keely, sort of, had come back again. Maybe "new and improved" was a better way to describe her.

A few weeks after my oral report, she had pulled me aside in the schoolyard one morning before the bell rang and informed me that my report had been the catalyst in helping her put things back in perspective. "I want to use my bad experiences to become a better person and to help people, just like Abraham Lincoln did," she had said.

Now she was nearly crazed in her desire to become a doctor, throwing herself into her studies, especially science, with such a vengeance that she was close to surpassing even Howard in her brilliance.

But along with the transformation, she was no longer my second best friend. Now Mary Washington was her best friend, and Althea Conley her second best friend. As for me, I had slipped so far down the ladder that we were really acquaintances more than friends. I guess that was okay since Mary and Althea were both black, and—by osmosis—they seemed to be inspiring the black part of Keely to rise to the surface. She no longer wore her hair in a Marlo Thomas flip. Like Alfreda, she cropped it closer to her face and kind of poofed it up, like Diana Ross sometimes wore hers on *The Ed Sullivan Show*. The three of them, Mary, Althea, and Keely, would sway together on the playground and emulate the dance movements and songs of The Supremes.

About the only lasting remnant of her fight with Bertha was that Keely's left eye had developed an involuntary spasm. One of our neighbors had the same mannerism, and I asked Grandmom about it one day. She told me it was a nervous tick. That made sense to me.

Since Keely's voice and hands no longer trembled like they used to, I assumed all her anxiety had been funneled into her left eye. Somehow, that seemed a better place for it.

It was near the end of April when Bernard began raising a clenched fist high into the air on the playground, proclaiming "Black Power." He kept quoting somebody in the news by the name of Stokely Carmichael that none of us had ever heard of, except him. "Stokely Carmichael says that the secret of life is to have no fear," Bernard chanted. "Stokely Carmichael says that the highest law is the law of conscience."

All this philosophizing proved to be too much for Robbie Taggert. When Bernard began reciting his quotes the next day at recess, Robbie yelled at him to shut up and called him the "N" word. It escalated into a fight, both of them winding up with a bloody nose and a consequent paddling.

Ezra had given me two more reasons to believe in life after death. March's reason was ghosts. "If life doesn't go on after death," he had said, "how come there are so many ghost stories?"

That was a dumb reason, and I told him so. With the hunt for Lincoln's ghost in the auditorium having turned into such a bust, I was pretty much fed up with any mention of ghosts. Ghost stories were all a bunch of hooey, I declared.

"Maybe so," Ezra said with a shrug.

"Well, do *you* believe in ghosts?"

Ezra just smiled at me with that raised-eyebrow expression he always made when he knew something I didn't.

April's reason sounded more like Ezra, much more philosophical and rational. God was eternal, he said. And so, if we were made in God's likeness, like the Bible assured us that we were, then we must be wired for eternity too.

I told him I would go home and think about that one, really hard.

Also during April, we were growing more and more excited about our impending sixth-grade class trip to Springfield, Illinois, at the end of May, the culmination and celebration of seven long years at Abraham Lincoln Elementary School.

Mr. Banner explained that the school was going to charter two private buses, since both sixth-grade classes would be going on the field trip, which meant I could sit next to Alfreda. For the last few weeks in April, our class had been studying maps of the city of Springfield and plotting the details of our trip. We would be leaving from the front of the school on the last Friday in May, at 7:00 a.m. sharp. Once we arrived in Springfield, our tour would begin with a visit to Lincoln's home; then we would go to his law offices; and finally, we would conclude the day with a trip to the Oak Ridge Cemetery, where Abraham Lincoln was buried. It crossed my mind, just for a second, that Lincoln's ghost had been spotted many times wandering around his final resting place.

And, oh yes, one other thing happened in April. I turned twelve years old.

Chapter 21

The first day of May happened to fall on a Monday. *That's good news,* I thought, as I dressed for school that morning and noted the calendar. This month I didn't have to wait even one day to hear Ezra's next reason.

But he was being cheeky. Rather than give me this month's rationale for believing in life after death during the first week of the month like he always did, he told me I had to wait until the end of the month. "After you get back from your trip to Springfield," he said.

"But why?" I moaned, exasperated by the unanticipated delay.

"Because I have a really good feeling about your field trip," he said. "And I think that this month's reason—the best one of them all, by the way—is all tied into it. Just trust me, little girl, and be patient."

"Good feeling, how?"

But Ezra just smiled.

As the month of May wore on, I was consumed with mixed feelings. In some ways, I wished the month would fly by, not only so that I could hear Ezra's next (most special yet) reason for belief in the afterlife, but also because of my mounting excitement over our class trip to Springfield. I was marking off the days on my calendar at home, making big, black X's with Grandmom's laundry marker as each day passed.

The other part of me, however, wished that the universe would get stuck somehow and that this month would go on forever. May was the last full month of sixth grade. Next month, the seventh of June was slated to be our final day of school, except for Friday, two days later, when we would return to class just long enough to receive our final report card.

Leaving Lincoln Elementary School forever was a daunting prospect that seemed nearly impossible to comprehend in all its ramifications. In the fall, my classmates and I would become seventh graders at a strange new school, Central Middle School, where we would suddenly become the younger class again. From the stories I'd heard, the eighth graders were sure to pick on us and make us endure all kinds of hazing rituals, like sticking signs on our backs that said "kick me" or guiding us to the bathroom or the janitor's closet when we asked for directions to our classrooms on the first day of school.

When it came right down to it, I loved everything about the old Lincoln School—the smell of it when you first walked through the front doors; the enormous oak trees surrounding all sides except the back playground; the old, white porcelain drinking fountains; the tiny, colored mosaic tiles on the floors around the back doors. I knew every square inch of this school, every spot where the hardwood floors creaked, all the teachers, most of the kids. For seven long years, over half my life, Lincoln School had been like a second home, sometimes even more of a home than my real home, at least during Grandmom's Geritol days or those aching times when she would clutch me against her chest and implore me not to grow up.

Middle school would mean that I was blatantly ignoring Grandmom's pleas—breaking her heart as I began wearing nylons to school, straightening my hair like the big girls did, and maybe even dabbing on a touch of makeup here and there, at least pink-pearl frost lipstick.

Central Middle School was named "Central" for a reason: it was a feeder school, meaning that seventh and eighth graders from various schools in Castalia would be conjoined under its gigantic slate roof. The school sat on a whole city block by itself, halfway from downtown, on the opposite side of Castalia from Lincoln Elementary. The walk to school would be more than two miles each way. I'd have to wake up an hour earlier each morning and get home that much later.

Central Middle School meant that the world was getting bigger, more impersonal. It meant fighting to be heard and seen, especially for those of us who weren't an "est" of any kind—not the prettiest, or smartest, or strangest, or any of the "ests" that landed you on either the top or the bottom of the heap. Being the best Andrea Powell, like Ezra proclaimed, might work for Lincoln Elementary School, but I questioned whether it would be enough for a huge school like Central where I was bound to get lost in the shuffle.

But the worst part about going to Central Middle School would be Ezra. Though I tried to pretend to myself that there would still be time to visit with him and Seth come fall, I didn't know when those moments might be. His shop was closed on the weekends, and by the time I walked home from Central after school, his door would already be locked for the night.

Alfreda was much more optimistic about the changes to come, fantasizing about how cool we would be as seventh graders; how we would blossom into teenagers during our years there and maybe even be allowed to go on group dates; how fun it would be to have a different teacher for every subject; how we could wear shorter skirts, just like Twiggy and the other stars we read about in *Tiger Beat* and the other teen magazines.

I had to admit that the prospect of growing up alongside of John Malone was exciting. Sometimes I would even kiss my pillow at night, practicing for the moment when we might share our very first kiss, my pink-pearl frost lipstick gently smeared on his lips. If that unforgettable event was in my destiny, it most assuredly would happen sometime during my two years at Central Middle School.

Alas, the twenty-sixth day of May quickly arrived, the final Friday of the month.

Before I left the house for the day trip to Springfield, I carefully packed my purse. Grandmom had urged me to take plenty of Kleenex along, in case my allergies kicked up and the mucous came pouring from my nostrils. She also gave me a bar of candy in case my stomach gurgled and another one for Alfreda in case hers did. I also packed a small hairbrush, some money for emergencies, a pack of Juicy Fruit gum, and . . . John Malone's fishing hat.

By the time I reached the school at 6:45 a.m., the two buses were already parked at the curb, droning in idle, spewing gasoline fumes. Mr. Banner and Mr. Jackson were both carrying clipboards and checking our names off as we arrived, just like the first day of school.

"We're going to be boarding each bus in neat, single-file lines," Mr. Jackson announced, nearly shouting so that he could be heard over the heavy motors of the busses. "No pushing, no shoving, and no smarting off. If you get a window seat, fine. If you don't, that's life. Everyone got that? No whining allowed."

Next, he walked over to Mr. Banner, and together, the two of them began coordinating their class lists. After some private discussion between them and some more name checking, Mr. Jackson was ready to make his next pronouncement. "What we're going to do," he said, "is board the buses in alphabetical order. As I call out your name, you get in line. Everyone got that?"

"Anderson, Kathy," he began, droning out our names, last name first, one by one, until he finally reached the end of the L's. Mr. Banner made one more quick count before the long line was instructed to board the first bus.

What great luck, I thought, as the rest of us—last names M through Z—waited in front of the second bus. Not only would John Malone be riding in the same bus as me, but the odds were pretty good that Alfreda Phillips and Andrea Powell might be seated side by side, just as we had hoped.

And we were! Mr. Banner called out our names, one right after the next, and we hugged each other in delight. I didn't even mind that she was the one who got the window seat.

A few rows ahead of us, Carol Martin had been assigned to sit beside John, which neither one of them was happy about. The little snitch had gotten on his nerves one time too many, and now she was whining that he had gotten the window seat. Had it been the other way around, she would have summoned Mr. Banner in an instant since he had implicitly stated that no whining was allowed. John crossed his arms and turned a cold shoulder against her.

The bus hissed into gear, and the driver began turning the large, heavy wheel away from the curb. His name was Mr. Jostic. I knew that only because he had a little nameplate over his head that identified him. After his name were the words "safe, reliable and courteous."

We were on our way. The two-hour drive to Springfield was peppered with more than thirty choruses of the Name Game song (one verse for every person's name on the bus), a rousing version of "100 Bottles of Beer on the Wall," and Jimmy Smithers's special rendition of "Stinkin' Lincoln" (sung to the tune of "Reuben, Reuben"):

"Stinkin' Lincoln, I've been thinkin'
What a great school you would be,
If the girls were all transported,
Into the Castalia sea."

When we arrived, standing in front of Abraham Lincoln's black-shuttered, two-story home was surreal. It almost felt like I was a time traveler, whisked back one hundred years, or like I had climbed inside of my history book. Not only had we seen numerous pictures of the home during class, but also we had studied every aspect of Lincoln's life in Springfield. Kathy O'Connor's oral report had quoted Lincoln's farewell address to the citizens of Springfield just before he had boarded the train that took him to Washington, D.C., where he would be sworn in as the sixteenth president of the United States.

"My friends," Lincoln had said that day back in February 1861, "no one, not in my situation, can appreciate my feelings of sadness at this parting. To this place, and the kindness of these people, I owe everything."

I could imagine his sorrow. Maybe leaving Springfield behind felt, to him, a little like leaving Lincoln School did to me.

Lincoln's home stood in the middle of a four-block historic neighborhood, restored to nearly exactly how it had looked back in the 1860s. Our tour guide was a young woman with wild red hair sticking out from beneath a bonnet tied beneath her chin and a mass of freckles across her cheeks and nose. She was dressed in a period costume like Mrs. Lincoln might have worn, but it looked silly on her—too frilly and refined for her tomboy walk and gestures. "Abraham and Mary Lincoln acquired this house in 1844," she informed us as Mr. Jackson smacked Robbie on the shoulder for pushing Bernard. "They purchased it from the minister who had married them two years earlier, Rev. Charles Dresser."

For some reason, the image popped into my head of Father Bob marrying John's parents. I looked at him quickly, wondering if he was thinking the same thing. He didn't seem to be. In fact, he didn't even seem to be listening. Instead, he was staring straight up toward the second-floor windows of the Lincoln home, his eyes squinting against the sun.

"When the house was built," the tour guide continued, "it was much smaller than you see today. It was only one and one-half stories. But the Lincolns enlarged the home to two full stories in 1856 to accommodate their growing family. Three of their four sons were born here, and one of them—Edward—died here in 1850 at the age of four . . . Shall we enter?"

We clamored around the front doorway, stopping in front of the door where a little brass nameplate read, "A. Lincoln."

"Since Springfield homes were not numbered until 1873," the tour guide explained, "the Lincoln family used this nameplate to identify their home to visitors."

As she swung the door open, our group began pushing to get inside. "Lines, please!" Mr. Banner snapped, tugging Jimmy Smithers back into single file. "If we all try to pile in at once, no one's going to see anything!" Meanwhile, Mr. Jackson was trying to bring some semblance of order to the rear of the line.

Alfreda and I were stuck somewhere in the middle of the commotion. It was downright annoying to be touring the home with such a large group. It was difficult to see, difficult to hear. But from what I could manage to see, I was struck by how dark the home was and how tiny the rooms were, by the gaudy patterns of the carpets and the wallpaper, and by the oppressive, velvet curtains hanging in nearly every room. It reminded me of the funeral home where the wake for my parents had been held.

The back parlor of the home was where Eddie had died, just before his fourth birthday. Being in any room where someone had died invoked a reverent, if not somewhat spooky, feeling. I pictured Eddie's chest rising as his little lungs drew in their last breath and imagined the sobs and moans of Lincoln and Mary echoing throughout the home. Did Eddie's soul travel up to the ceiling and then out through the window and up toward heaven? I looked up at the ceiling. Maybe it happened that way if there really was life after death. I wondered what Ezra's next reason would be.

The sitting room was full of garish pinks and greens and patterns and textures that all seemed to clash with each other. This room was like the family room of today, the tour guide explained. She said that the Lincoln family relaxed in this room—Lincoln usually stretched out on the floor because the furniture wasn't comfortable enough to accommodate his large frame. This was also the room where Fido, the family dog, spent most of his time. Fido was given away to a neighbor, she said, when the Lincolns moved to Washington. I thought about how hard that must have been for Willie and Tad to part with their beloved dog. We'd even seen a picture of Fido in one of our textbooks.

"Unfortunately," Howard said, "Fido was also assassinated." There were gasps all around as Howard continued his story. "One day, Fido jumped with his dirty paws on an old drunk who was sitting on the curb. The man pulled out a knife and stabbed poor Fido to death."

Everyone was shocked, including the tour guide, who looked at Mr. Banner with bulging eyes, like Ricky Ricardo's.

"Yes, I'm afraid that's a true story," Mr. Banner said with a shrug, giving the startled tour guide a half-sheepish, half-proud smile. "Our class has been studying Lincoln history—um—very thoroughly this year."

After the shock of Fido's untimely demise began to fade, I shifted my concentration to the smell of the old house. It didn't smell like anything in particular, which was a surprise, especially since the rooms were so dense. When we traveled upstairs to the second floor and I brushed my fingers against the banister, I could hardly believe that my hand was actually touching the same wooden surface that Abraham Lincoln's hand used to touch on a daily basis.

The weirdest thing about the Lincoln bedroom to me was the sight of his bed. It seemed way too small for a tall man like him. I imagined his enormous feet dangling out from the end of the mattress, his long, bony toes twitching under the moonlight.

It felt good to be outside again, back in the fresh spring air and the light of day. Being stuck so far back in line as we toured the house, I had missed a lot of information from the tour guide. Someday, maybe Grandmom and I could come back to Springfield, I told Alfreda. It would be much more fun to tour the home again when we weren't traveling with more than sixty noisy sixth graders. Alfreda agreed.

"But I thought the house was a dump," she said. "Dark and depressing! If I never see it again, it'll be too soon!"

The day wasn't turning out to be the trip of a lifetime that I had envisioned. Boarding the buses to tour the next destination became a gigantic production each time, complete with clipboards, check marks, single-file lines, and strict, alphabetical organization, not to mention the endless pushing and shoving among the boys.

The weather was getting hotter by the minute, and Bertha Riggs was overripe. The entire bus reeked from her stench. Besides that, my allergies were kicking in, just like Grandmom had feared. Good thing I had packed wads of Kleenex. Alfreda was bored with the whole trip. She confessed that Mr. Jackson had not inspired as thorough a study of Lincoln lore as Mr. Banner. "It was boring in class, and it's even more boring to see it in person," she said, sighing and picking her fingernails as we bumped along toward the final destination, the tomb in Oak Ridge Cemetery.

As for John Malone, I hadn't seen him even once, up close anyway, since we left the school. The closest I got was watching the back of his head on the bus. As we neared the entrance of the cemetery, his face was nearly pressed against the window, his back toward Carol Martin, who was haranguing him for obstructing her view on purpose.

For some reason, I started to wax philosophical as the buses came chugging to a halt. Here we were, tracing the steps of Abraham Lincoln's life, one century later. Maybe it was the impressive sight of his white granite tomb looming in front of us, but an odd, surreal feeling was taking hold of me, a little like that feeling I had experienced under the stage spotlights during the Christmas recital.

The shape on the top of the tomb was an obelisk, resembling the Washington Monument, rising in the center of the memorial more than one hundred feet into the air. I wondered what it would be like if I ever got famous, and one day, years from now, kids came traveling in buses to see the school that I had attended, the house where I had lived, the grave where I was buried. I wondered if there really was such a thing as reincarnation. Maybe that was what life after death was like—rebirth into another life on earth, no heaven at all. How would we ever know if we used to be somebody else? What if one of us in this very bus, maybe even Robbie Taggert, was really Abraham Lincoln reincarnated? I glanced toward the back of the bus at Robbie, who was making farting noises. It was a stupid thought.

Mr. Banner was standing outside our bus with his clipboard as we disembarked. Bernard was the last one to exit. "Okay, kids," Mr. Banner said, "this part is going to be a little different. There is no formal tour here. You can go around and tour the tomb at your leisure. We're going to be stopped here for an hour."

"An hour!" Carol Martin moaned. "What are we supposed to do here for a full hour?"

"There's a lot to see," Mr. Banner said, trying to be encouraging, but I could tell he was deflated, saddened by our lack of enthusiasm after all his hours of meticulous teaching. "The tomb has countless sculptures to look at and read about, both inside and outside." His feigned cheerfulness dissolved. "But if you get tired of walking around, I guess you can just come back to your seat in the bus and wait."

Alfreda exhaled a heavy breath. "Let's just go quick and see where he's buried," she whispered. "I brought my transistor radio along. We can go back to the bus after that and listen to WLS."

That was the only thing any of us really cared to see firsthand: Lincoln's actual crypt. Though there were dozens of sculptures and statues adorning the outside of the tomb, just like Mr. Banner had promised, all the kids went rushing inside at once like a wild stampede. Mr. Jackson looked at Mr. Banner with a sigh, tossing his clipboard to the ground.

What silly kids, I thought. *We have a whole hour to be here, plenty of time for everyone to look around at their leisure, and there they are, acting like a herd of buffalo.* I guessed it had become some kind of stupid race to be the first person to see Lincoln's tomb.

I remained standing with Mr. Banner and Mr. Jackson near the outside of the memorial entrance, watching Mr. Jackson light up a cigarette. Smoking made him look handsome, like the Marlboro man. Mr. Banner smiled at me. "Come here a minute, Andi," he said.

I did as he requested and followed him over to a huge bronze bust of Lincoln's face. "Look at this," he said. "This bust was created by Gutzon Borglum. The original stands in the Capitol building in Washington."

"He looks sad," I said, staring into Lincoln's bronze eyes. Actually, I was thinking the same thing about Mr. Banner, though I didn't dare say it out loud, especially since I felt somewhat responsible. Ever since Mr. Alphonse had resigned from teaching, Mr. Banner's face had dimmed a little more each day, as if all his inner lighting was slowly shorting out.

"Yes, he does look sad," Mr. Banner agreed. "Borglum actually used the life mask of Lincoln that we read about in class, the one Vorg made, to create this piece. So, I guess it's pretty much the way he really looked.

Borglum was the same sculptor who did the presidential faces on Mount Rushmore."

I continued to gaze into Lincoln's eyes.

"Go ahead, rub his nose," Mr. Banner said.

"Why would I want to do that?"

He laughed and said, "Everyone does it. Rubbing the nose on this sculpture is supposed to bring you good luck. That's why his nose is discolored. Anyway, rubbing the nose on this particular sculpture is nearly a legend in itself."

I giggled and then lifted my fingertips and swished them around Lincoln's bronze nose. I smiled at Mr. Banner and giggled again.

"Hope it works for you, Andi," he said with a grin.

I started to walk into the monument and then turned around and came back to Mr. Banner's side. "Why don't you rub his nose too?" I said. I figured Mr. Banner could use some good luck, especially after all we had put him through.

"Perhaps I will," he said, his face softening as he looked at me. "Thank you, Andi."

After that, I decided to take my time through the whole memorial and read about every single piece, especially since we had a whole hour to kill. I could listen to a transistor radio any old time.

Slowly, I entered the rotunda. I soon found myself moving inside the same narrow corridor the rest of the kids had rushed through a few moments before. Located in niches along the walls were various statues, depicting Lincoln from different periods of his life. Four bronze tablets on the walls were engraved with some of his most famous speeches, like the Gettysburg Address and a portion of his second Inaugural Address.

At last, I reached the heart of the memorial, the burial room. It felt eerie, especially when I realized I was standing all alone. The walls were black and white marble, and the ceiling was gold leaf. In the center stood Lincoln's coffin, encased in reddish marble. His name and the dates of his birth and death were etched on it. Nine flags surrounded the tomb. On the wall above the American flag was an inscription: "Now he belongs to the ages."

Everything was quiet in the room. My eyes were fixed on the red marble; Lincoln's dead body was only inches away from me. This was my chance, the chance of a lifetime. Closing my eyes, I whispered a prayer invoking the ghost of Abraham Lincoln to appear, once and for all. I popped my eyes open again and looked around.

Nothing.

It might help, I thought, if I could get even closer to him and actually touch his crypt while I said another prayer, but the velvet stanchions designed to keep tourists at bay blocked the way.

I did another quick scan of the room. Though I could hear the sounds of tourists, maybe kids from our class, reverberating way down at the end of the long corridors, I was still alone. Daring myself to do it, I crawled beneath the velvet stanchions until there was nothing but marble in between Abraham Lincoln and me. "Please, Abraham Lincoln," I whispered, "Please give me a sign that you're here." I reached out and stroked the red marble with my fingertips.

"What does it feel like?" said someone behind me.

I instantly recognized the voice of John Malone. My heart skipped, half from being caught in the act, half from being caught in the act by John Malone. "It just feels cold," I replied, crawling back underneath the stanchions to stand beside him.

"It's pretty cool in here," he said. "In this room, I mean. Don't you think?" His eyes were drifting up toward the gold ceiling. "You know, Lincoln's not really buried in that red thing you were touching. He's really buried in a cement vault ten feet below this floor."

"I know," I said. But I didn't really, until just then.

I suddenly had other, more important things on my mind than Abraham Lincoln. John Malone and I were standing together. *Alone together*. It was the perfect time, the perfect moment, and given our history, the perfect place. I opened my purse and reached inside until I found his fishing hat. "Here," I said, handing it to him.

"*My* hat?"

I nodded.

"Where'd you find it? I thought for sure it was long gone."

"I went back to the school early one morning. And I found it. You know, the morning after we . . . went searching for Lincoln's ghost."

"And you've had it for that long?"

I nodded. "I didn't want to give it back to you in front of other people. I didn't know how that would look, how to explain it."

"Cool!" He smiled and slipped the white canvas hat back on top of his head and pulled it down over his eyes. His whole body seemed to relax.

"John, I really like you." I could hardly believe how unexpectedly those words had just tumbled out of my mouth. They seemed to echo in the high-ceilinged space.

"I know," he said, lifting up the rim of his hat again, his brown eyes intent on mine. "But you deserve somebody better than me, maybe someone like Howard. He'll probably end up being an accountant or somebody important. But not me. I'm no good."

"But I don't like Howard," I said. "I like *you*."

He shrugged. "That's just 'cause you don't know me. If you knew me, I mean, really knew me, you'd stay away." He stuffed his hands in his pockets and started to enter the corridor on the other side of Lincoln's burial room.

"John!" I called out. "I've got something else to tell you."

He stopped. Turning around slowly, as if he was debating whether he should, he finally came back over to where I was still standing in front of the marble sarcophagus.

"I *do* know you," I said. "I was in the bait shop the day that you told Ezra all about Father Bob. Ezra didn't know I was there. I was hiding. Anyway, I heard the whole story."

To my surprise, though his body stiffened at the mention of Father Bob's name, he didn't get angry or anything. He just stood there, his eyes glazing over like he was disappearing somewhere, the toe of his penny loafer scraping against the floor.

"John," I said. "I think you are the bravest boy in the whole world to do what you did."

"Then you believe me?"

"More than that," I said. "I believe *in* you."

His eyes snapped into focus again, and he looked at me, his dark eyebrows furrowed, almost as if he was trying to figure out who I was. Or what I was. We could hear the accelerating noises of tourists in the distance coming down the corridor in the direction of the burial room. And then, in one quick movement, something happened that I would relive over and over again, on the bus ride home and all through the summer, wondering if it had ever really happened at all or if I had only imagined it.

John Malone leaned over—and kissed me on the lips.

Though it must have taken half a second, time began moving in slow motion as soon as I realized what he was planning to do. I know they say that you're supposed to shut your eyes to make it more romantic, but I couldn't bring myself to do it and miss the moment. I wanted to see him up close, the expression on his face, savor the softness of his bangs crushed against my own forehead. His eyes were closed, but mine were wide open.

Chapter 22

By the time the bus arrived back at Lincoln School and hissed to a bumpy stop near the front curb, I had already relived John Malone's kiss dozens and dozens of times in my head. In spite of what had happened between us, John had turned around to gaze at me only once during the entire, long ride home. When our eyes met, his lips rose in a faint, half-smile, and then he looked away again.

I thought my heart would break inside of me—from joy, of course. Yet still I was surprised to discover that utter joy could hurt as much as it did. Grandmom always cried at the happiest moments in movies—like at the end of *It's a Wonderful Life*, when the entire town bailed Jimmy Stewart out of his debt, ZuZu's petals were snug in his coat pocket, Clarence was getting his angel wings, and everyone was giddy with joy. Still, something about that part of the movie was always the hardest for me to watch. That's what I was feeling right now, a joy so deep that it ached.

As we disembarked from the bus, dozens of parents had already arrived, in cars or by foot, eager to claim their children, making the scene in front of the school one of general merriment and chaos. You could hear the sounds of happy chatter as my classmates relayed their stories about the trip.

I looked at my watch. I thought about visiting Ezra at the bait shop, but it was already well after six o'clock. Although the sun would not be setting for another couple hours, a golden haze streamed through the clouds, casting a dewy yellowish glow on everything.

Grandmom was not waiting for me, but I had not expected her to be. It was Friday, her bingo night. I was actually glad for a moment of privacy after spending so many hours with a large, noisy group. Walking home, in solitude, would provide me one final opportunity to reflect on the memory of this beautiful day before the sun went down on it forever.

As I neared my house, I could hardly believe who I saw coming down the street in my direction. *Rubbing Lincoln's nose for good luck must really work*, I thought quickly. First, John Malone's kiss, and now this! Straight ahead, strolling right toward me, were Ezra and Seth. I had never seen them on the white side of Lincoln School before.

Ezra was wearing one of his cream-colored linen shirts, and his long, thick dreadlocks were cascading down his back; Seth, untethered by a leash, kept in perfect step with his master. With their syncopated, graceful pace and the way they flowed together, they seemed like two separate pieces of the same work of art.

"Ezra!" I shouted, running toward him. "I'm so happy to see you! I couldn't wait to tell you my news, and now I don't have to wait! You are not going to believe what happened to me today! John Malone *kissed* me!"

"Hallelujah—you finally got that seed planted!" He flashed a wonderful smile, his white teeth bright against his mocha skin. "Didn't I tell you something good was gonna happen? Didn't I tell you that life is seeds?"

"You were right!" I beamed. "You're *always* right, Ezra!"

"Try to hang onto the feeling you have right now. Feelings don't get any better than that."

"I will," I said.

"And never forget, there ain't nothing—nothing at all—that's stronger than love."

Ezra had never looked handsomer to me than he did right then at that moment, standing beneath the pre-sunset sky, the muted sunlight shining on his skin and hair, his eyes the color of honey. Seth's coat, too, seemed to be glistening in the dreamy light.

"In the depth of your hopes and desires lies your silent knowledge of the beyond," he said. "And like seeds dreaming beneath the snow, your heart dreams of spring. Trust the dreams, little girl, for in them is hidden the gate to eternity."

I stared at him, puzzled. Although I'd heard him talk in his strange riddles countless times before, something seemed different about him. I couldn't quite put my finger on it, but the sight of him mesmerized me in a brand new way. "What does that mean?" I asked.

"I just quoted you some lines from a book called *The Prophet*," he said. "It's by Kahlil Gibran. Read it sometime."

I nodded.

"You promise me?"

I nodded again.

"Okay then," he said. "Seth and I got to be getting on home now."

"I'll see you next week, Ezra!" After they were a few feet away, I suddenly remembered something.

"Ezra!" I called out. "You were supposed to give me this month's reason when I got back from Springfield. Remember?"

He stopped, turned around, and looked at me long and hard. "Andi Powell, what on earth you doing out here in the dead of winter dressed like that? Put your coat on, little girl, and hang on! Spring'll be here before you know it." Then he smiled his dazzling smile again but didn't say one more word.

I did not find out until the next day, Saturday, when Alfreda came to my house, a trip she'd never made before, actually crossing the imaginary boundary line of Lincoln School just to appear at my front door.

"Did you hear the awful news yet?" She was sobbing.

"What awful news?"

"Ezra and Seth were both shot and killed yesterday afternoon while we were in Springfield! The bait shop was set on fire! When the firemen rushed in, they pulled out both of their dead bodies. Nearly the whole bait shop was burned to the ground!"

Chapter 23

The last day of sixth grade and the day after Ezra's funeral, we gathered together in Mr. Banner's class one final time to retrieve our report cards. John and I had not spoken a word since Lincoln's tomb. The news about Ezra had pretty much sent him completely adrift.

Afterward, clutching my report card, I stood at the top of the front steps outside, waiting for him. As he raced passed me, still wearing his fishing hat, I called out his name, and he stopped.

He would not look at me as I spoke. I told him all about seeing Ezra and Seth after they were killed, every single detail about the way they looked and what he had said. Up close, John's eyes had a horrible, painful look in them that never went away once throughout the telling of my story. At its conclusion, he said simply, "I'm glad you finally got to see a ghost. For Ezra's sake, I hope the next life is better than this one."

And then John Malone ran away from me, into the promise of a summer that would never come.

That day, the final day of sixth grade, was thirty-seven years ago.

"It doesn't seem possible, does it?" I said now to John Malone's coffin. The grave diggers who would come to plant him in his final resting place still had not arrived.

I wondered why and when I had stopped loving John Malone, but it was a moot point. By the time we began seventh grade, John was already lost—to me and to everyone else. The day he arrived at Central Middle School, he was reeking of that sweet, musty scent that I would later come to recognize as the smell of marijuana cigarettes. By high school, he appeared dazed most of the time, his dull eyes veiled behind an assortment of drugs that most of us could only guess about. One time in English class, he started picking imaginary bugs out of the air and having a conversation with himself. He was sent down to the school nurse and didn't return to school for days.

I realized, now, that I had been one of the last people on this earth to glimpse the true essence of John Malone before he began his slow, bewildering descent into self-anaesthetization. Still, it had taken nearly forty years to completely kill that sweet, defiant spirit.

Times were much different now. Just recently, Father Bob had been among countless Catholic priests across the country who had made the headlines. Apparently, after being transferred away from St. Matthew's the same summer that Ezra died, Father Bob had gone on to molest boys in three more parish schools. It was a pity that neither of John's parents was still alive now to read the news.

The Catholic Church, however, continued to stand behind Father Bob, even after all the allegations, choosing to transfer him to an administrative position within the hierarchy of the church rather than try to make restitution or atonement for his deeds. If abortion of the unborn was a sin, what about abortion of those already existing? It was staggering to think of the dozens and dozens of John Malones whom the actions of Father Bob had single-handedly eradicated.

Ezra had been right, as always; John Malone *was* a hero. Even all these years later, not the lawyers, the countless testimonies, or the billions of dollars spent on legal fees and victim payoffs could topple the mighty Father Bob. And yet, one brave little boy had once had enough faith to believe he could do it all alone.

The grave diggers were now in sight, off in the distance in their truck, soon to begin their appointed task. As I bent down to kiss his coffin, it suddenly occurred to me that I had never stopped loving John Malone after all. I could almost feel his peace, like a vibration, seeping through the sealed lid and enveloping me in its mist, as if his liberated spirit was encircling me. I had absolutely no doubts or fears about life on the other side of the grave. Ezra's beautiful ghost had seen to that. *This* side was the one to mourn.

But I knew what Ezra would say about that too. This side is merely winter, he would say. Stay strong, and don't deny the spring.

This side is seeds, dreaming beneath the snow.

Epilogue

After sixth grade, my life became a journey, of sorts, strewn with mixed blessings. I'll just share some highlights.

From middle school on, I turned most of my attention to my schoolwork. I studied hard enough to earn a scholarship to college. Later, I went on to graduate school and then received my PhD. For the past fifteen years, I've been a professor of comparative religion at a Chicago university.

Though I've struggled with depression my entire life, I've experienced equally impressive moments of utter joy to create an interesting balance. Throughout my career, I've authored a few books, including *Ten Reasons to Believe in Life after Death* and *Lincoln and God*. I'm working on a new book now: *The Book of Ezra.*

There have been some men who have mattered to me along the way, but each of them ended up, eventually, belonging more with someone else. And I have attended some churches along the way. But for me, God has been too big to be contained within the walls of any of them.

Alfreda and I have remained lifelong friends. Right after high school, she and Bernard got married, moved to California, and brought ten children into the world. Though we live on opposite sides of the country, we no longer allow boundary lines—imaginary or otherwise—to separate us, and we get together at least twice a year. One of our most memorable reunions occurred several years ago, when we made the trek to Indianapolis to participate in a ceremony honoring Mr. Banner as statewide Teacher of the Year, shortly before his retirement.

I was fortunate to be able to be with Grandmom, at her bedside, on the morning she died. I was still in college at the time. Moments before she heaved her final breath, her eyes popped open with ecstasy, her arms outstretched upward toward the ceiling. "Mary Jane!" she cried out.

After college graduation, I finally got my first dog—a German shepherd of course, named Hank. Though he died many years ago, his was a good seed. His grandson, Zachary, similar in color and markings to Seth, is my dog right now.

Lincoln Elementary School was torn down in the mid-1970s. Built in its place was a new steel and glass structure, and the school was renamed Herman B. Greene Elementary School, in honor of the man who had originally donated the land. There's never been, to my knowledge anyway, another supernatural sighting of Abraham Lincoln since.

Besides John Malone, I never told another living soul about seeing Ezra's ghost.

The very day that Alfreda informed me that Ezra had died, I walked to the public library to check out the book *The Prophet*. I needed to fulfill my last promise to Ezra as soon as I could.

Since that day, I have never been without a copy of the book nearby. And whenever I feel lonely for Ezra, or just lonely, I simply read it again.

And so it was that I brought the book with me to the cemetery that day and read these final words aloud to John Malone before he was planted into the earth:

"And if our hands should meet in another dream, we shall build another tower in the sky."